"*Angel,*" *Vittorio whispered.* "*Angel, what are you trying to do?*"

She shook her head. She didn't know.

He released her carefully, half expecting her to fall, but she stepped back and looked at him with the bleakest expression he had ever seen. He couldn't bear to look at her.

"Why do you want me to think badly of you?" he asked.

"You will anyway, whatever I do," Angel said sadly. "It's safer this way. Go on thinking the worst of me, Vittorio. It's probably true."

She walked out of the room, leaving him stunned.

He tried to tell himself that everything was very simple. She'd just confirmed his worst suspicions. But he couldn't make himself believe it.

Harlequin Romance®

presents

international bestselling author

# LUCY GORDON

**Readers all over the world love
Lucy Gordon for powerful emotional drama,
spine-tingling intensity and Italian heroes!
Her storytelling talent has won her countless
awards—including two RITA® Awards!**

Escape to the beauty of Rome with
Lucy Gordon's upcoming story:

*One Summer in Italy...* (#3933)

On sale in February 2007—
this story is definitely one to look out for!

# LUCY GORDON
*Married Under the Italian Sun*

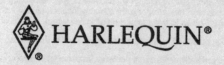

# HARLEQUIN®

TORONTO • NEW YORK • LONDON
AMSTERDAM • PARIS • SYDNEY • HAMBURG
STOCKHOLM • ATHENS • TOKYO • MILAN • MADRID
PRAGUE • WARSAW • BUDAPEST • AUCKLAND

ISBN-13: 978-0-373-18257-2
ISBN-10:      0-373-18257-0

MARRIED UNDER THE ITALIAN SUN

First North American Publication 2006.

Copyright © 2006 by Lucy Gordon.

This edition published by arrangement with Harlequin Books S.A.

® and TM are trademarks of the publisher. Trademarks indicated with
® are registered in the United States Patent and Trademark Office, the
Canadian Trade Marks Office and in other countries.

www.eHarlequin.com

Printed in U.S.A.

**Lucy Gordon** cut her writing teeth on magazine journalism, interviewing many of the world's most interesting men, including Warren Beatty, Richard Chamberlain, Roger Moore, Sir Alec Guinness and Sir John Gielgud. She also camped out with lions in Africa, and had many other unusual experiences that have often provided the background for her books. She is married to a Venetian, whom she met while on holiday in Venice. They got engaged within two days.

Two of her books have won the Romance Writers of America RITA® Award: *Song of the Lorelei* in 1990, and *His Brother's Child* in 1998, for the Best Traditional Romance category.

You can visit her Web site at www.lucy-gordon.com.

# CHAPTER ONE

'LADIES AND GENTLEMEN, here we are again with your favourite TV programme, *Star On My Team*, when the famous—and sometimes the infamous— ha-ha!—team up with *you* to win fabulous prizes...'

Sitting backstage, Angel prayed for the burbling introduction to be over soon. In fact, she thought, please let the whole mindless business be over. Just as her marriage was over, and only awaited a decent burial.

The presenter was getting into his stride.

'On my right, Mr and Mrs Barker, and their famous team member—' He named the star of a minor soap opera. Watching the backstage screen, Angel saw him enter, flashing his teeth and grand-standing to the audience.

Nina, her personal assistant, surveyed her with critical approval.

'You look perfect,' she said.

Of course she did. Angel always looked perfect.

That was her function. Long blonde hair, large, dark-blue eyes, slender figure encased in a tight gold dress, cut teasingly low. Masses of glittering, tasteless jewellery. *Bling, bling!*

'And now, the lady I know you're impatient to see—'

*Not as impatient as I am to finish this,* she thought wryly, while trying to remain good-tempered. *Time to get out there. Big smile!*

'The one we've all been waiting for…'

*Especially since my husband plastered my face all over the front pages, trying to divorce me on the cheap. Never mind. Smile!*

A look in the mirror, a final adjustment of her dress to ensure that her assets were displayed to advantage, mouth widened just so far, no further. And now for the last walk to where the lights beckoned and the cameras preyed on her. It felt like a walk to the guillotine.

'Here she is. The beautiful, the fabulous— *Angel!*'

She'd done this a hundred times before, and it should have been easy, but as she emerged and the applause washed over her, something terrible happened. The lights seemed to dim, and suddenly her mind was filled with darkness and panic.

*Please, not now! I thought those attacks were over!*

Mercifully, the dreadful moment passed swiftly. She could cope again, just.

She advanced on the suicidally high heels, hands outstretched, voice tuned to a note of artificial ecstasy to greet the presenter.

Her fellow contestants were Mr and Mrs Strobes. She'd met them in the hospitality room before the show and it had been an endurance test.

'We're so sorry about your divorce,' Mrs Strobes had said. 'We think it's just terrible the way he threw you out.'

'Parting was a mutual decision,' Angel had hastened to say.

But what was the point, with Joe flaunting his new companion at every party and nightclub?

The audience was agog to see her, so she smiled and waved, turning this way and that so that they shouldn't be disappointed. She could almost hear the comments.

'A right sexy little piece—a bit of all right.'

That was what her husband had wanted from her. For him she'd been a 'right sexy little piece' for eight years, and suddenly eight years felt like a very long time.

The show started. The questions were ridiculously easy, but even so she gave a performance of racking her brains, giggling at her own 'ignorance'. They wanted 'dumb blonde' so that was what she would give them.

The soap actor on the other side seemed to be genuinely dumb, and Angel's team was soon in the lead. The clincher came when the host burbled, 'And now, Angel, here's a real tough one for you. Who painted the Sistine Chapel? Was it a) Maisie the Mouse, b) Michelangelo, or c) Mark Antony?'

She did her bit, putting her dainty fingertips to her mouth and giving an 'Angel' giggle.

'Ooh, dear! I don't know. I never studied music.' Roars of laughter from the audience. 'Could you repeat the question, please?'

He did so and she gave a little squeal.

'You always give me the hard ones. I'll have to guess. Michelangelo.'

'Michelangelo is right, and you have won.'

Cheers, applause, her team mates bouncing with joy. It would be finished soon. *Cling to that thought.*

At last it was over and she could escape. Nina was waiting for her with the car, so that she could make a speedy escape from all the prying eyes.

Nina had been with her for eight years, secretary, maid, gofer and good, solid friend. She was a little younger than Angel, plain, funny, and a rock to cling to.

When they were on their way, Angel let out a long sigh of relief.

'At least that's over,' Nina said. 'With luck you'll never have to do another one.'

'Not once I'm living in Italy,' Angel agreed. 'Amalfi, here I come.'

'I really wish I could come with you.'

'So do I,' Angel said, meaning it. 'I'll miss you, but I shan't need a secretary, even if I could afford one now. I'm going to live a very quiet life.'

'Joe called me today and asked me to go back to work for him. He said "darling Merry" needs me. Merry! I ask you. Her name's Meredith.'

'And mine's Angela, but I let him rename me Angel for the sake of his image.'

'I told him I'd found another job. As though I'd work for him again—a great, stupid vulgarian who thinks he's somebody because he's rich.'

'Mind how you talk about my ex-husband,' Angel said mildly.

'You object?'

'Certainly. "Great, stupid vulgarian" doesn't begin to do him justice.'

'How about, "coarse, spiteful, bullying thug"?'

'That's much better,' Angel said with a wry little laugh.

'You're well shot of him. And, even if he did cheat you out of a proper settlement, you got an Italian palace out of it.'

'The Villa Tazzini isn't a palace. If it had been, "Merry" would have wanted it. He bought it for her, but without letting her see it first. It was to be a wonderful surprise. But when she realised it wasn't palatial, just a large country house, she didn't think it was wonderful at all.'

'Rumour says it cost him a million.'

'A palace would have cost at least five million. I heard he showed her a lot of pictures he'd taken, and she ripped them up.'

'I suppose Freddy told you that,' said Nina, naming Joe's PA, who was secretly on Angel's side, as was everyone who'd worked for her.

'That's right. Apparently her language would have made a stevedore blush.'

'And Joe let her talk to him like that?'

'She's twenty, and sexy. It boosts his ego to flaunt her—'

'Next to his fat, forty-nine-year-old self?'

Angel laughed. 'Next to his fifty-two-year-old self, actually. But that's a secret. Even I only found out by accident. But the point is that as long as Merry does him proud, she can talk to him how she likes. Anyway, he finally tossed the place to me and said, "You can have that as your divorce pay-off. Take it or leave it."'

'And that's *all*?'

'I get a lump sum as well, but I'll have to be careful with it. It'll cover my expenses until the lemon harvest comes in. Part of the estate is an orchard, and when I sell the crop I'll have enough to get by.'

'Even so, you could have fought Joe for a fair share. With his millions he's got off cheap.'

'I know, but he could have tied me up for years, fighting him and his army of lawyers. I simply felt very tired, so I took it. After all, I've always loved Italy.'

Once, she'd planned to study art at college, then go on to Italy to study some more. She'd even learned Italian. But that dream had come to nothing, when her beloved grandfather had fallen ill and needed her.

Now, ironically, she was going to Italy after all. But not to Rome or Florence, the centres of art. Her new home was a villa on the Amalfi coast where the cliffs plunged dizzyingly down to the sea.

Anything was worth it, she told herself, if she could still take care of the old man who had offered her a home after her parents died when she was eight. They had been strangers, not having seen each other for five years.

'Hello, I'm Sam,' he'd said, refusing to have any truck with that 'talking down to kids nonsense', as he had called it. And Sam he'd been ever since.

They had been poor, and life had been a struggle, but they loved each other, and when Sam's health had failed all she'd cared about was looking after him. For a while she had had a boyfriend, Gavin, who had dazzled her with his handsome looks, but she had broken up with him when he made it clear there was no place for Sam in their lives.

Hoping to win a little money, she had applied to enter a television quiz show. That was how she had met Joe Clannan, a shareholder in the production company that made the show. He was a property millionaire, and, when he had proposed, she had accepted for Sam's sake.

Joe wanted a young sexy trophy wife, and he made her change her name. To him, 'Angela' was dull and provincial, but 'Angel' was the sexy, young 'bit' that he wanted.

He took her to every film premiere, every fashionable restaurant opening, and she was always dressed to the nines and dripping with jewels. The idea was to show the world that coarse, vulgar Joe Clannan had a wife that other men envied him for.

She did what pleased him because she was grateful that Sam now had a comfortable life with her, cared for by two nurses. Often he didn't know who she was, but he seemed happy, and that was all she asked.

She became a minor celebrity, famous for being famous, appearing on reality TV, fluttering her eyelashes, giggling and doing all she could to make Joe proud.

But when she became pregnant Joe showed his true colours. He already had two grown sons from a previous marriage, and he wasn't keen on Angel losing her figure. He even suggested that there was 'no need to have it'. That provoked a fierce row in which she stood up to him so determinedly that he never mentioned it again.

But it was all for nothing. Two days later, she miscarried. In the weeks of depression that followed, she became, as he put it, poor company. He found a younger woman, a girl of twenty. He reckoned Angel was past her best, at twenty-eight.

She had always known that beneath the surface bonhomie Joe could be a very unpleasant man. Just how unpleasant she discovered during the divorce, when he drove her and Sam out of the house and gave her as little as he could get away with.

She cared nothing for the money. If it weren't for her grandfather, she would have thought herself well rid of Joe.

After the hideously gaudy mansion in the heart of London's West End where she'd once lived— 'Nothing too good for my Angel!'—she now rented a small house on the edge of town, just big enough for herself, Sam and the two nurses. She'd taken it on a short-term lease, and in a few weeks she must have the Villa Tazzini ready for them all.

On the night before she left for Italy, she dropped in to Sam's room.

'I'll be leaving very early tomorrow,' she told him.

'Why are you going away?' he asked, puzzled.

'Darling, I told you. I'm going to Italy, to see this house where we're going to live. It's my divorce settlement from Joe.'

'Joe who?'

'You remember Joe—my ex-husband.'

He frowned. 'What became of Gavin?'

'We quarrelled. Never mind all that now. We're going to have a new home in Italy. Look, here are the pictures of it that I brought you. You'll come and join me as soon as possible.'

He fixed her with the smile she loved, full of warmth and affection.

'Why are you going away?' he asked.

Vittorio Tazzini was waiting at the window, watching the street for the moment when his friend appeared. As soon as he saw Bruno he was at the door, almost pulling him inside.

'Have you got it?' he asked eagerly.

'Vittorio, my friend, I'm still not sure this is wise. You're obsessed, and that isn't good.'

'Obsessed! Of course I am. I've been cheated by two men: the first was one I called a friend, until he stole from me and vanished, forcing me to sell my home to pay his debts. *His* debts, Bruno, that he had persuaded me to sign for. The other was Joseph Clannan, who saw my desperation and used it to beat me down on the price. I sold for much less than the place is worth because I needed money quickly. If I could have got a fair price I'd have had enough to give me some hope for the future. I wouldn't be penniless and living *here*.' He cast a scornful look around the shabby rented room that was his home now.

Bruno regarded him with pity, which he was careful to conceal. They were both thirty-two, and had been friends since their first day at school. Nobody knew the fierce, embittered

Vittorio better than his gentle friend. Nobody understood him as deeply, or feared for him more.

He was silent, watching Vittorio pace the narrow confines of the room, his tall, rangy body looking so out of place in it, after the spaciousness of the Villa Tazzini, that it was like seeing a wild animal trapped in a tiny cage. Sooner or later the animal would go mad.

Vittorio wasn't a handsome man. His face was too harsh for that, his cheeks too gaunt, his eyes too fierce. His nose was irregular, so that people meeting him for the first time wondered if it had been broken. His wide, firm mouth suggested an unyielding nature, one that could love or hate with equal ferocity, and never forgive an injury from foe or lover alike.

Even Bruno, his closest friend, was slightly afraid of him, and pitied anyone who got on Vittorio's wrong side.

'Won't you forget that man for a moment?' he begged now.

'How can I forget him?' Vittorio asked savagely. 'He forced the price down until he practically stole the estate from me! And do you know why? To impress a woman. To make her a gift of my home at the least possible expense to himself.'

'You don't know that,' Bruno pleaded.

'But I do. As I showed him round I heard him

say, "My pretty lady will just love this. It's just what she said she wanted." All for a woman. So now I want to see that woman. You said your friends in England could send you something that would show her to me. Do you have it or not?'

'Yes,' Bruno said, reluctantly unwrapping the small parcel he carried. 'This is a video of a television show called *Star On My Team*. It was shown last week, and they taped it for me. But I still wish you'd drop this. Hate the man if you must, but why blame *her*?'

'Do you think they can be separated? Do you think I don't know the kind of woman who puts a price on the bedroom door, and then ups the price again and again? We all know them. Give me the tape.'

Taking it, he pressed it into an ancient video recorder that stood in the corner of the room, poured two glasses of wine, and the two of them sat down to watch.

*'Here she is. The beautiful, the fabulous—Angel!'*

Vittorio never took his eyes off the ravishing blonde, with her long hair, luscious make-up and a sexy pout, as she sashayed out to meet her audience.

Flaunting herself, he thought cruelly, taking in the golden figure-hugging dress and flashy jewels. A woman used to being waited on, who demands the best, and gets it.

'*Putana,*' he muttered. Prostitute.

'That's going too far,' Bruno protested.

'You think a wedding ring hides what she is?'

'She may not be wearing it any more. My friends say there is talk of a divorce.'

'So she demanded my home as her parting present? Is that supposed to make me feel better?'

At that moment, Angel gave her famous inane giggle. It went up the scale, growing more lush and significant with every teasing note. She put her fingertips daintily over her lips, looking from side to side as if to say, *Silly me.*

A perfect performance, Vittorio thought. Apparently fatuous, but actually calculated to tempt a man through his weakness. Even he had felt a faint tingle up his spine, and it served to increase his rage.

Bruno stared at Angel's polished beauty.

'She may be all you say,' he mused, 'but you can see why—'

'Oh, yes,' Vittorio said contemptuously. 'You can see *why*!'

There was a tinkling sound as his wine glass broke in his hand, crushed by the cruel pressure of his fingers. He seemed unaware of it. His eyes were fixed on the screen, and the beautiful, pro-vocative woman laughing as though she didn't have a care in the world.

The journey began with a flight to Naples. It would have been easy to call the villa and ask for someone to collect her from the airport, but getting there under her own steam seemed a good way to start her new, low-profile life. Besides, Angel liked the idea of arriving unexpectedly and seeing the house as it was naturally.

It was an impulse she soon regretted. Being in-dependent was fine if you had only a few bags. But if you were carrying all your worldly goods it was a pain in the neck to have to load them into a taxi at Naples airport, unload them again at the railway station, then onto the train to Sorrento, followed by a bus to Amalfi. By the time she was in the last taxi, to the villa, she was frazzled.

But she forgot the feeling as she gained her first glimpse of the dramatic Amalfi coast. She'd heard of it, and studied pictures, but nothing could have prepared her for the dazzling reality of the cliffs swooping down, down, down into the sea.

'They're so high,' she said in wonder. 'And those little villages clinging to the sides—how come they don't slide down into the water?'

'They are protected by a great hero,' the driver

announced proudly. 'The legend says that Hercules loved a beautiful nymph, called Amalfi. When she died, he buried her here, and placed huge cliffs all around to safeguard her peace. But then the fishermen protested that they would starve because now they couldn't get to the sea, so he built them villages on his cliffs, and vowed that he would always keep them safe. And he always has.'

Looking down, Angel found the pretty tale easy to believe. What else could explain how the little towns clung on to the steep sides, rising almost vertically, white walls blazing in the sun?

'Is the Tazzini estate up there?' she asked.

'Right on top, although the lemon orchard stretches down the cliff face, in tiers, to catch as much sun as possible.'

'Are the lemons good?' she asked, trying to sound casual.

'The best. The makers of limoncello always compete to buy Tazzini lemons.'

'Whatever is limoncello?'

'It is a liqueur, made with lemons and vodka, straight out of heaven.'

So she had a ready market for her produce, she thought, with a surge of relief.

'There they are,' the driver said suddenly, pointing as they rounded a bend. 'Those are lemon flowers.'

Angel gasped and sat totally still, riveted by the sight that met her eyes. It was as though someone had tossed a basket of white blooms from the top of the cliff so that they cascaded down, shimmering, gleaming, dazzling in the sun, awesome in their beauty.

On the last stretch she took out a mirror and checked her appearance. She'd resolved that those days were behind her, and in future she would worry less about her appearance. But she simply couldn't let her first entrance be less than perfect, and so she checked her mascara and refreshed her lipstick. Now she was ready for the fray.

They were approaching a large pair of wrought-iron gates which were closed but not locked, so the driver was able to open them and go through. Another few minutes and she could see the villa.

As she'd told Nina, it wasn't a palace but a large country house, although built on impressive lines. Made of pale grey coloured stone, it reared up three floors, with a flight of stairs running up to the second floor from the outside, where a covered balcony ran the length of the building. Down below there was a riot of decorations. Little half-fountains appeared out of the walls, watched over by stone animals carved to incredible perfection. Angel found herself smiling.

Three broad steps led up to the double doors that formed the entrance, and which stood open. She went right in, followed by the driver, who was hauling her many bags. Looking around, she saw a hall that was spacious yet strangely domestic, even cosy. Warm red tiles stretched away across the floor, leading to archways that seemed to invite her in. Incredibly, she felt welcome.

She tried to be sensible. This feeling of having come home to the place where she belonged was the merest sentimentality, sugar coated with wishful thinking. Yet the sensation pervaded her, despite her efforts to resist it. It was almost like being happy.

She paid the driver, refusing his offer to carry the bags further. She wanted to be alone to enjoy her first minutes in this lovely place.

From the hall a flight of stone stairs with wrought-iron banisters streamed upwards, beckoning her. Angel began to climb it slowly, feeling as though she were moving in a dream. Halfway up she stopped to look out of a window, and realised that the house was close to the edge of the cliff, directly overlooking the sea. From here she could see the water stretching into the distance, incredibly blue, shining serenely under the clear sky. The window was open and she stood there a moment, breathing in the clear air, listening to the silence.

When had she last heard silence? When, in her rackety life, had there been such peace, such potential for tranquil joy? If she hadn't come here, how much longer would she have survived?

Soon she began to climb again. After the heat outside, the house was blessedly cool, protected by the thick stone walls. She emerged onto a large landing, leading to a corridor with several doors. One in particular attracted her attention, because it was the only double door. No doubt this would be the master bedroom, and the one she would take as her own.

Eager to see it, she pushed open both doors and walked in.

For a moment she could discern nothing, as the wooden shutters at the three windows were mostly closed. Then the gloom cleared slightly and she saw that one of them was open a few inches, and a man was standing there, looking out through the narrow gap.

At first Angel could make out little of him, except that he was tall and lean. Then, as her eyes grew accustomed to the gloom, she saw that he was dressed in old jeans and a frayed denim shirt, with scuffed shoes to complete the picture.

Probably the gardener, she thought. But what was he doing here?

'Hello?' she said.

He turned quickly.

'Who are you?' they both said together, in Italian.

Angel gave a brief laugh, realising that her indignation was a tad illogical.

'I'm sorry, this is my fault,' she said, 'for not letting anyone know I was coming today.'

He pushed the shutters further open so that light streamed into the room, falling directly onto her like a spotlight as she moved towards him. She saw him grow suddenly tense, his face harden, but he didn't speak.

'I'm the new owner of the estate,' she said.

'The Signora Clannan.'

Angel had reverted to her maiden name, but she let it go for the moment.

'That's right. Obviously you've been expecting me.'

'Oh, yes, we've all known you were coming, although not exactly when. You kept that detail to yourself, so that you could catch us unawares. Very shrewd. Who knows what discoveries you might have made?'

She could see him better now, and thought she'd never come across any man who looked so hard and unyielding. There was a gaunt wariness about him, not just in his face, but in his tall, angular shape, the way he crossed his arms defensively over his chest, telling the world to keep its distance.

He might as well have warded her off with a sword, she thought.

'I wasn't trying to catch anyone out,' she said, trying to remain good-tempered. 'It was an impulse decision.'

'And you couldn't even have made a phone call from the airport to give Berta a chance to be ready for you? She's your housekeeper, and a more faithful, hard-working soul never lived. She deserves better.'

Angel had a faint sense of remorse, but it was quashed in the rush of indignation. What the hell did he think gave him the right to talk to her like this?

'Look,' she said, 'I presume you're one of my staff, so let me make it clear right now that you don't speak to me like that. Not if you want to go on working for me.'

'Is that so? Then how fortunate that I don't work for you, or I'd be shaking in my shoes now.'

'Don't be impertinent. If you're not one of my employees, what are you doing in this room, where you most decidedly have no right to be?'

She thought he grew a little paler, the twist to his mouth a little more sardonic.

'True,' he said. 'I have no right. Not any more.'

'What do you mean?'

'My name is Vittorio Tazzini, and I used to own this place.'

# CHAPTER TWO

'You?' The word had an unflattering tone that came out before Angel could stop it.

'Yes,' he said, looking down at himself. 'A scarecrow like me. This used to be my room, and I returned to search for something I left behind. I apologise for being here when the new *padrona* arrived. If I'd been warned, I'd have cleared out and not troubled you.'

She was disconcerted, not so much by his words as by the way his eyes flickered over her. There was nothing new in that. For years men had gazed at her with admiration, even frank lust, trying to strip her in their thoughts. She had thought she was bored by it, but it might have been better than the contempt in this man's gaze.

'There's no need to be melodramatic,' she said coolly.

'Is it melodramatic to call you *padrona*? Isn't that what you are? The new mistress to whom everyone will now defer? I'm merely recognising reality.'

'No, you're trying to make me feel uncomfortable, as though I should be ashamed of being here.'

'It never occurred to me that you would feel ashamed of anything.'

'Look, this won't work. I've seen off sharper men than you.'

'I don't doubt it. Your very presence in this place is a triumph. But what will you do now you're here? I'll wager you haven't given it a thought. Not a serious thought, anyway. But why should you care? Those huge alimony payments will take care of all problems.'

'Not that it's any of your business,' Angel said, her eyes beginning to sparkle with anger, 'but I intend to make my own way. I understand the estate is profitable. Everyone assures me that Tazzini lemons are second to none.'

He regarded her sardonically.

'So, you've heard about the lemons and now you think you know everything.'

'No, but I know about limoncello.'

A grin spread over his face, suggestive of derision rather than amusement. It made her uneasy.

'Truly,' he said, 'your knowledge is awesome.

But how far does it go? For instance, what kind of lemons are grown in this place?'

'What kind? Lemons are lemons, aren't they?'

'You instruct me. How foolish of me not to think of that.'

'Now, look—' she began hotly.

'Lemons, as you so expertly say, are lemons. But are they Meyer lemons, Eureka lemons, Lisbon lemons?'

'All right. I didn't know there was more than one type,' she said, facing him squarely.

'No, and you don't know which kind is the best for limoncello. In fact, you know nothing.'

'Well, I'm not planning to tend them myself. I'll employ someone who knows what to do. In fact, there must already be someone working here.'

His grin became a little wild.

'You have nobody who can care for those lemons so that they'll get the best price,' he said flatly.

'There are gardeners, aren't there?'

'There's one. He's a good workhorse, but he's not an artist. You'll have to explain everything to him.'

'But surely there's a head gardener, who doesn't need to be have things explained?'

'The only one who knows is me, and I'm out of here since you seized my home.'

'You're blaming me? You've got a nerve. Is it my fault you chose to sell?'

'I did not—' He stopped himself with a sharp breath. 'Don't trespass on that situation. You know nothing.'

'Then don't throw accusations at me. I didn't seize your home—'

'No, your husband did. But who ended up owning it?'

'And that makes me a criminal, does it? I have no desire to "trespass on that situation" as you call it. I just want to take over my new home and settle in.'

He drew a sharp breath.

'As you say,' he said coldly. 'Welcome to *your* home. I'll inform your staff that you're here.'

He walked out, followed by her glare. If there had been anything to throw, she would have thrown it.

She was furious with him for ruining the first special moments here. Everything had been peaceful and beautiful, until she'd walked in and found him waiting, almost as if trying to spring a trap for her.

It was no use telling herself that it had been pure accident. That was common sense, and she wasn't in the mood for it.

In fact, she was annoyed with herself for acting

like Angel at her most queenly and petulant. She'd believed that was part of the old life, left far behind. But years of being pampered and deferred to had left their mark, despite her best intentions.

I have not allowed Joe to turn me into a spoilt brat, she reassured herself. I have *not*.

Well, perhaps just a bit.

Angel strode to the other two windows and pushed the shutters wide open so that sunlight streamed in everywhere, like a benediction. Now she could look around the room, which was like no bedroom she had encountered before. Like the rest of the house that she had so far seen, the floor was covered in dark red flagstones. The bed was almost seven feet wide, with a carved walnut headboard and matching foot.

Trying it cautiously, she found that the mattress was firm almost to the point of hardness, but when she stretched out for a moment it was curiously comfortable. The lamp on the bedside table was defiantly old-fashioned, with a carved stand and a parchment shade.

There were two wardrobes, also of walnut, standing in the spaces between the windows. Ornate on the outside, they were basic on the inside, with rails and wire hangers, so unlike the padded satin hangers on which her elegant clothes normally hung. A large chest of drawers stood against one wall.

And that was it.

And yet she felt at home. The very starkness and simplicity of the room was peaceful.

Angel delved further into one of the wardrobes, realising how old it was, and how much in need of repair. The floor actually had a hole. Reaching into her bag, she took out a small torch that she carried everywhere and trained it on the hole. The light went right through to the floor, showing her something small and green.

Reaching under the wardrobe, she managed to grasp the object, which turned out to be an address book. Perhaps this was what he'd lost. He must have left it in a trouser pocket, from where it had fallen out of sight.

From down below she heard a woman's voice, sounding worried, almost tearful, then Vittorio Tazzini's, seeming to comfort her. She just managed to get to her feet and brush her clothes down before the door opened and a powerfully built middle-aged woman entered, with Vittorio's arm about her shoulder.

'This is Berta,' he explained in English. 'She looks after the house and does a wonderful job.' He translated this for the woman before reverting to English to say, 'Unfortunately, she understands very little of your language, and she's worried in case this counts against her.'

'Why should it?' Angel asked. 'We can speak in Italian.' She crossed her fingers and spoke slowly. 'Berta, I'm sorry that I did not warn you I was coming. It was rude of me.'

To her relief, Berta understood, and a smile broke over her broad face. She too spoke slowly.

'If the *signora* will come down to the kitchen I will prepare coffee while the room is made ready.'

As they descended the stairs, Angel could see that the household was already alive to her presence. All the staff were buzzing around her bags, beginning to take them upstairs, but not before they'd given her quick looks of curiosity.

She could sense the other woman's unease, and it touched her heart. She hadn't come here to hurt anybody.

When Berta served up coffee, Angel thanked her with her warmest smile and said in slow, clear Italian, 'This looks delicious. I'm sure we're going to get on really well.'

Berta nodded, looking happier.

'By the way, is this what you were looking for?' she asked Vittorio, holding out the little book.

'Yes, it was. Thank you. Where did you find it?'

'It had fallen through a hole in the bottom of one of the wardrobes.'

Berta tut-tutted. 'There now! Such a state some of the furniture's in! But you'll be able to see to it, won't you?'

To Angel's surprise, this was addressed to Vittorio.

'Why should you say that?' she asked. 'Now that Signor Tazzini's property has been found I see no reason for him to come here again.'

Berta's hand flew to her mouth. 'Oh, dear! You haven't said—'

'Haven't said what?' Angel asked, her eyes kindling.

'It's only—you knowing nothing about the estate,' Berta faltered, 'and the *padrone* knowing so much…'

'Perhaps you'd better leave us for a moment, Berta,' Vittorio said quietly.

'*Si, padrone.*'

It was the word '*padrone*' that reduced Angel's patience to danger level. Berta had called him 'master' because that was how she still saw him. And the way she scuttled out underlined the unwelcome fact.

'Do you mind telling me what's going on?' Angel said coolly. 'Because everyone seems to know, except me. In fact, you seem to have made quite a few decisions that I know nothing about. Perhaps it's time you informed me.'

'All right, it's very simple,' he said in a hard voice. 'You need an estate manager, a real expert, and that means me. You haven't a hope of doing it on your own, you've already proved that.'

'Damned cheek!'

'Well, face facts. You don't know the first thing about the lemons you grow, not even what type they are. How often do they need watering? How long between planting and harvesting? How often do they flower? The whole prosperity of this place depends on intensive knowledge, or your harvest will fail. And I didn't spend years working myself to a standstill to see you throw it away.'

'If that's your way of asking me to hire you, you're making a very bad job of it.'

'Don't waste my time with that sort of talk. I'm not *asking* you to hire me. I'm telling you. You don't have a choice.'

'The hell I don't!'

'That's right, you don't. You need me, that's the plain fact, so why waste time?'

'And you did it all on your own, did you? Without you there's no one except the "work-horse" you mentioned?'

'No, I had a staff of three gardeners, but they've gone except for that one. The other two left when the place was sold.'

'How interesting! They both made the same sudden decision, did they?'

'They did.'

'And both left on the same day?'

'In the same hour.'

'What a remarkable coincidence! I wonder exactly how it came about.'

Her ironic tone left no doubt of her meaning, and Vittorio's eyes darkened.

'You mean, I take it, that I encouraged them, in order to harm you?'

'It seems pretty clear.'

He moved towards her so suddenly that she couldn't stop herself from taking a step back, although it maddened her to yield so much as an inch. She found her back against the wall.

'Listen to me,' he said, in a soft, deliberate voice, full of menace. 'You are very confused about what is clear and what is not clear, so I am going to make several things *clear* to you.'

'This conversation is over,' she said, trying to move sideways and away from him.

But he stopped her by placing both hands on the wall, on either side of her.

'No, this conversation is not over until I say so,

and *I* have decided that there are things you must hear first.'

'And I say I don't want to, so you will move away and let me go right now.'

'Will I, indeed? And who is going to make me? You? Try it.'

She would have been mad to try. Even though he wasn't actually touching her she had a fierce sense of the wiry strength in his body, and knew that she was no match for him. To fight would merely be undignified.

His eyes were fixed on her face, following her thoughts exactly. He grinned, and it was an alarming sight.

'Nor will any of the others help you against me. Do you think they will?'

Dismayed, she knew the answer. In the eyes of the household, he was still the master.

'So you will stay here and listen to me, and when I am quite sure that you have understood I will let you go.'

'Then get it over with,' she said through gritted teeth.

'The first thing is this. You have accused me of being prepared to damage this place because of my contempt for you. I told you before, I put my life's blood into the estate and hell will freeze over before I do anything to harm it. What you suggested would be an act of petty spite, and it's an insult that I won't tolerate.'

'Then perhaps you should have heard yourself say it,' she flung at him. 'You were delighted to have caught me out. Admit it.'

'Of course I admit it. But I didn't catch you out. You caught yourself out, thinking you could come out here and take over when you know nothing. Your arrogance is unbelievable. That's why they left, because they are knowledgeable men and they don't sell their services to ignorance. Expecting them to do so was your insult to *them*. They wouldn't tolerate it, and why should they? You think I drove them away? On the contrary, I begged them to stay. Not for you, but for the estate, for the earth and the things that grow here, that need tending and loving, and which are more important than their pride, or yours.' He took a shuddering breath. 'Or mine.'

The last words sounded as though they were wrenched out of him. For a moment his attention seemed to wander, as though he'd side-slipped into another world. Then he forced himself back with an effort.

'Just so that you understand, I do not descend to acts of spite, and I won't tolerate the way you just spoke to me. Don't ever do it again or you'll be sorry.'

'And that's supposed to make me hire you, is it? Threatening me?'

'You need me, damn you.'

'I don't think so. You've got the thing you came to find, so now get out of here. Do you hear me? Get off my property.'

Angel spoke bravely but her heart was hammering at what she could see in his face. For a moment she thought Vittorio would lose control, but at the very last second he mastered himself. A shudder went through him. His hands fell from the wall and he moved away from her. She had a strange feeling that his strength had suddenly drained away.

'Your property,' he said bitterly. 'Yes, it's your property now. I wish you joy of it.'

'Liar!' she flung at him in a shaking voice. 'You wish me nothing but misfortune and misery.'

'How astute of you!'

'Get out of here now, and don't come back.'

He gave her one final look of hatred. Then he was gone.

Angel had expected a disturbed night but, to her surprise, she slept like a log. The apparently hard mattress was the most comfortable she'd ever known.

Awaking early, she found the room still in

darkness, but with slivers of light creeping between the cracks in the shutters. Pushing one of them open, she saw the softly growing light of early dawn. Entranced, she watched the sea, so still that it had an unearthly quality.

It was perfect, she thought, smiling.

Almost perfect.

The fly in the ointment was Vittorio Tazzini, a dangerous man who had taken against her in a way she didn't understand. True, she owned the home that had once been his, but she hadn't stolen it. Perhaps he hadn't wanted to sell, but had been forced to by debts. Even so, he must have money left over, enough not to have to dress in such a down-at-heel manner.

He was a mystery, but one she didn't intend to let worry her. She'd thrown him out. Now she must put him out of her mind. It should be simple enough.

But it wasn't; she knew that already. He had the kind of presence that wouldn't be easily dismissed. He wasn't handsome—well, not in the ordinary way, she corrected herself. His nose was too prominent, his mouth too grim, his cheeks too lean for conventional good looks. What he had was all his own, a kind of dark inner force, unforgiving, implacable. He would be a bad enemy.

Yet she wasn't afraid of him. Far from it. For

years the men she'd met had been too much alike—smooth, full of glib talk and meaningless compliments, all seeming to come from the same insipid mould: photographers, television producers, minor actors, models, young men with little personality but the kind of regular features that passed for good looks, flashing cheesy smiles, always performing with one eye on her, the other on the camera, and their inner eye on the impression they were making.

She'd almost forgotten what the genuine article was like until she'd been forcibly reminded by a man who smelled of the earth after rain, and had no pretty speeches, only a blunt ferocity that, however disagreeable, was, at least, honest. Their encounter had left her strangely exhilarated.

By closing her eyes she could conjure him up again, leaning close, his hands pressed against the wall on either side of her. She knew he hadn't touched her, not by so much as a fingertip. How, then, could she explain the sensation of his hands roving all over her? She could almost feel them now, yet it had all been in her mind.

I've got to pull myself together, she thought, almost amused. If my life had been half as colourful as the press thought, I'd be handling this better.

It was too soon to get up for the day. She went

back to bed and fell asleep again, but this time she had strange dreams. Footsteps walked through her head, although she could see nobody. She heard the steps going away and knew that she must stop them or something terrible would happen. But, before she could do anything, she awoke.

Breakfast was on a balcony overlooking the sea, a magic place where small birds came daringly close and even landed on her table, demanding crumbs. She became so entranced with them, and the sight of the impossibly tiny boats below, that she almost forgot to eat.

Berta served her delicious coffee and rolls. At first she was reserved, as if her loyalty was still to Vittorio. But gradually she thawed under Angel's determined friendliness.

They spent the rest of the day exploring the house and Angel's delight grew. She loved this place. She even loved its slight shabbiness, its lack of pretension.

It had seen better days, as was shown by the light patches on the walls where pictures had been removed. The bathrooms were pure nineteenth century, with pipes that clanked but delivered gallons of hot water. She was entranced.

'It was built four hundred years ago, for…'

Berta named a once notorious ducal family. 'Their main residence was a palace, but this was created for a younger son, who brought his bride to live here. After that, it passed to a daughter, then to her daughter. It's been several generations since anyone with a title lived here, but it's been a happy family house.'

It was on the tip of Angel's tongue to ask why Vittorio had had to sell, but she stayed silent, feeling sure Berta would pass the question on to him. Hell would freeze over before she let him guess she was curious about him.

Not every picture was gone. Some of the walls bore murals, and she spent some happy hours studying them, recalling everything she had ever learned about art history.

Angel found a suite of rooms that would be ideal for Sam and his carers. It was downstairs, as climbing was becoming too much for him, and would give him a large, pleasant room looking out onto the garden on the landward side of the house, with his nurses nearby.

She made a mental note of the furniture she would have to buy, and how much redecorating would be needed. For the moment, she told Berta only that the rooms should be spring-cleaned. More detailed explanations could wait until she felt more able to take Berta into her confidence.

She also began to walk her estate, which was more extensive than she had realised. In addition to the lemon orchards, there was a huge garden, stretching away landward, built on several levels, connected by short flights of stone steps. Flowers of every kind grew in profusion—roses, geraniums, magnolias. There were fountains with water plants, and greenhouses with tropical plants. Rico, the only gardener left, came with her, explaining that it was arranged that something different would flower every month.

Angel had begun to understand why Rico, alone among the gardeners, had chosen to stay. He was sweet-natured and always willing to please, but his mind worked at a snail's pace. He had been born on the estate, lived there his entire twenty-three years, and plainly knew that he wasn't fit to venture out into the big, bad world.

Vittorio was his god. Angel began to feel that if he said, '*Il padrone* always used to…' just one more time, she would do something desperate.

Once she caught Rico off-guard, looking about him and clearly wondering how he was going to manage all this alone. Angel felt exactly the same. There was a horrible feeling growing inside her that Vittorio Tazzini was laughing at her. With good reason.

Another day, Angel went walking alone along

the cliff top, where an iron rail guarded her from the drop. After a couple of hours she stopped and lingered, enjoying the sun that bathed her and glittered on the sea below. Cautiously, she peered over the rail at the long drop. Far below she could see the beach, with sun umbrellas and boats drawn up at the water's edge. At this distance the bathers looked no bigger than ants. Fascinated, Angel rested her hands on the rail and leaned forward.

There was no warning of what happened next. She felt the movement of earth beneath her feet and the next moment she was sliding away under the railing, going down, lashing out frantically for something to grab.

For one terrifying moment, she thought there was nothing. Then her fingers touched metal and she tightened, and held on. She managed to reach up her other hand and clench that too on the railing, but her relief lasted only a split second. She'd checked her descent, but she was hanging over a sheer drop.

'Help!' she screamed. *'Help!'*

But she might as well have been in the middle of a wilderness. Nobody on the estate knew that she was here, and it was unlikely that anyone could see her from so far below. Even if they could, it would take time for help to arrive, and she wasn't sure how long she could cling on.

*'Help!'* she screamed again. It might be useless, but she couldn't stop.

Still, there was nobody to help her.

She fought to get a foothold, but her legs scrambled uselessly in space. She was already running out of energy because, with her arms stretched above her head, it was hard to breathe. Now sheer terror attacked her, making breathing even harder.

She cried out again, but the wind whipped her words away and brought no answer. She would simply hang here for hours, unnoticed by anyone, until exhaustion overtook her and she fell.

# CHAPTER THREE

ANGEL CRIED OUT AGAIN, and this time it wasn't a word but a long scream of agony.

*'All right, I'm coming.'*

At first she wasn't sure she'd heard the words. The wind snatched them away, then returned them in an echo.

'Help!' she screamed again, frantic with hope and fear.

But she could hear no reply. She'd imagined it. Nobody was coming to help her, and very soon she would be dead.

'I'm here.'

The next moment a head appeared above her. She thought she was hallucinating as she saw it was Vittorio, but he dropped to his knees, then lay flat on the ground.

'All right,' he called. 'Don't panic. Here—'

He was reaching out his hand, wrapping his fingers around her wrist where she was still gripping the iron rail. Then the other hand, so that he held both wrists.

'You're going to have to let go of the rail,' he said.

'I can't—'

'You must,' he said patiently. 'I can't pull you up while you're holding it. Trust me.'

But her fingers seemed frozen, defying her will to move them. While she fought to make herself do what she must, there was an ominous crumbling sound, and a little more of the cliff slipped away beneath her. Looking up, she saw that most of it had come from the ground where he was lying, leaving a big hole beneath his upper body.

'Don't think about that,' he said, his face just above her.

'How can I? You're lying on nothing.'

'The hole gives me more room to pull you up. Be positive and trust me. Let go of that rail.'

Gasping, she did so, and immediately felt his hands tighten on her wrists, drawing her up, into the gap that crumbled further as she went through. He was inching back slowly—slowly—until he reached a place where he could draw himself up to his knees. As he did so his forearms were forced to take more of her weight, causing his fingers to tighten on her wrists. She gasped at the sheer power of that grip, and, with her eyes fixed on his face, she could see the terrible strain it cost him.

'One more heave,' he gasped.

On the words he yanked back sharply, so that Angel slid swiftly through the gap beneath the rail and landed on the ground, feeling it blessedly firm beneath her body.

She was safe, but that was only a word, and it had no power against the gasping and shuddering that seized her.

'Oh, God,' she whispered. 'Oh, God!'

He put his arms right round her, pulling her hard against the length of his body and holding her there without moving or speaking. She clung to him in return, knowing that if he let her go she would start screaming. She tried to stop herself shaking but it was useless. The safety of the ground beneath her was an illusion, and only he could keep her safe.

'Are you all right?' he asked after a while.

'No,' she said abruptly. 'I think—I'm going to have hysterics. Sorry about that.'

'Don't be sorry,' he said, almost impatiently. 'Nothing wrong with hysterics. Have them if you like.'

After that nothing could have stopped her. Her gasps turned into whooping, her shaking became violent tremors, and tears poured helplessly down her face. It didn't seem to faze Vittorio. He just tightened his arms, so that an already firm grip became one of steel.

There was nothing gentle or tender about this. It was less an embrace than an imprisonment, but that was what she needed to guard herself from the worst, until the world became steady again, the storm passed and she managed to say, 'Damn, damn, damn! I thought I had more guts than that.'

He loosened his grip just enough to look at her face. His own was close enough for her to feel his breath fanning her lips.

'Why?' he asked mildly. 'You were a hair's breadth away from falling to your death. Has that ever happened before?'

'No.'

'Then why should you think you should cope?'

'Well, we both know now that I can't,' she snapped, furious with herself and, obscurely, with him.

'So what? Did someone pass a law saying that you had to be a superwoman? Or is that just what the rest of us are supposed to think?'

'Will you shut up?' she snapped.

He grinned. 'That's better. Come on. You're ready to stand.'

She didn't feel ready, but he seemed to know

her better than she did herself, so she allowed him to help her to her feet.

'Where's your car?' he asked.

'I walked.'

'Then it'll have to be my car. It's just over there.'

His car was small and shabby. Angel eased herself thankfully into the front passenger seat, closed her eyes, and didn't open them again until they pulled up outside the villa.

'The *padrona* needs a good, stiff drink,' Vittorio told Berta, who bustled out.

'We both do,' Angel said, leading the way into the large room that opened onto the garden through tall windows.

Berta produced whisky and two glasses, and Vittorio poured for them both. Angel drank hers in one gulp.

'Do you need another?' he asked, holding out the bottle.

'No, thanks. I don't normally drink spirits at all, but this was different. Thank goodness you were there. How did that happen?'

'You mean how dare I still be on your property after you ordered me off?'

'Not exactly. After all, you saved my life. I owe you for that.'

'You don't owe me any favours. It wouldn't

have suited me at all for you to die. Everyone would have thought I'd murdered you.'

His brisk, common-sense manner was a relief. There would be no need for melodramatics along the lines of, *My hero!*

'Surely not!' Angel said ironically. 'Why would anyone think you wanted to murder me? I know you hate the sight of me, but who knows about it—apart from everyone in the area?'

He grimaced. 'All right, you've made your point.'

'Then tell me, what *were* you doing there?'

'I went to look at the cliff.'

'You *knew* it was dangerous?'

'Only since late last night. Rico called me and said he'd noticed that it was dangerous at that point. He didn't know what to do.'

'He could have told me.'

He gave her an ironic look.

'The poor lad is scared stiff of you. He came to me because that's what he's always done. I said I'd check it today, and that's why I was there. I was going to cordon it off, then come to inform you.'

'Oh, you *were* going to let me know what was happening? But only after you'd checked it.'

Vittorio let out his breath in exasperation.

'All right,' he said, with exaggerated patience.

'Just tell me what you'd have done. How would you deal with a crumbling cliff?'

The silence was jagged as they faced each other.

'You want me to say I'd come to you, don't you?' she seethed.

'I don't care what you say, only what you do. I hope you'd have had enough common sense to call me, but I don't count on it.'

'You've got a nerve!'

'It depends whether you love this place more than you resent me.'

She sighed. 'You've got me there, haven't you? After all, *you* love it more than you resent *me,* or I wouldn't be alive now. I guess I have to respect that.'

'Much against your will, of course.'

She spoke through gritted teeth. 'Look, I'm *trying.*'

'I know. It's years since I enjoyed anything so much.'

'All right, have your laugh. But please come and look after the estate before it goes to rack and ruin. That is—if you can bear to.'

'I can bear to. I told you once before that taking care of the land is the only thing that matters. Next to that, nobody's feelings count. I'll do a good job for you, and get your lemons in prime condition for the harvest, but I must have a free hand, and you have to take my advice.'

She opened her mouth to protest about this high-handed way of putting it, but then closed it again. He was right. She had no choice.

'All right,' she said.

'My first piece of advice is to get the other gardeners back.'

'No, it's not fair to leave it all to Rico, is it?' she agreed. 'Plus, he helped to save my life.'

'True. You should give him a bonus. There's a heavy workload, not just for the lemons, but the rest of the garden. You sell that produce as well, at least you will sell it if it's properly tended.'

'Can I leave it to you to contact the other two gardeners?'

'Certainly. And my second piece of advice is that you need some fertiliser delivered fast.'

'Please order it. Is this a truce?'

'I suppose it is.'

'Don't strain yourself,' she said indignantly. 'We can make it an armed truce if you prefer.'

'That might work better.'

'How much do I pay you?'

'I'll send you a formal memo.' He added with a faint smile, 'Under an emblem of crossed swords.'

'Surely *sheathed* swords is more appropriate?' Angel asked lightly.

Vittorio regarded her, his head on one side, his smile unreadable.

'Let's see how things work out before we sheath our swords.'

Angel slept badly that night. As soon as she closed her eyes, she was back hanging over the drop. Somehow she knew that this was a dream, but would struggle to save herself, feeling certain that she could now manage without him. But Vittorio was always there, hauling her back to safety.

Then she was lying on the grass again, held against him, gasping and feeling her heart pounding. That was when she awoke to find it was still happening, and she would have to calm herself down before she could go back to sleep. But she seemed to be stuck in a loop of terror and excitement that repeated again and again, until she faced the truth—that she had wanted to feel his hands on her. In fact, she had wanted it ever since the first day in the kitchen.

'It ought to be enough that I dislike him,' she muttered crossly, when she'd woken up for the third time. 'You'd think that would protect me.'

But there were some things against which there was no defence.

That kind of consciousness, Angel discovered,

was an insidious thing. It didn't leave you alone for a moment. It was there even when a man was talking to you with barely concealed impatience, without even looking at you properly, all his attention directed at the papers he was spreading out. You might try to concentrate on the figures he was explaining, but you couldn't help noticing the shapeliness of his hands, or remembering their unexpected power. And afterwards you wouldn't be able to recall any of the figures.

The gardeners were re-employed and Vittorio brought them to be introduced to her. In a private talk afterwards, he told Angel what he had promised them in wages, and what she would be paying him. She had an odd feeling that he was accepting less than he was entitled to, but his distant manner forbade her to mention it.

The gardeners were polite to her, but there was no doubt whom they regarded as their real employer. In fairness, Angel had to admit that they had a point.

'Is all this agreeable to you, *padrona*?' Vittorio finally asked.

'I've put everything in your hands, and I won't go back on my word.'

He gave a brief, wry smile. 'Of course not, since it would not be in your own interests to do so.'

'Meaning that you think I couldn't be trusted otherwise?'

'Meaning that I have the highest regard for your intelligence. Now, if you'll excuse me, your servants will get to work.'

'Don't give me that nonsense,' she exploded. 'You're no servant and we both know it. You're getting a kick out of this, aren't you?'

'If you really believe that, *padrona*, perhaps you'd like to change your situation for mine.'

She had no reply, and after a moment he moved away, leaving her mentally kicking herself.

She watched the three of them walking across the grass, and she couldn't help but notice how easily he moved. The other men were clodhoppers by contrast, but he was like a prince, with an easy, languid grace that was a pleasure to behold.

But she would still keep out of his way, Angel decided. Every conversation was like duelling with a thorn bush.

Not that she avoided him entirely. It was only sense to watch him at work and learn how the estate functioned. She told herself that she was guarding against the day he would decide to walk out.

Vittorio found himself as content as he could ever be as a servant in the place where he had been master. Angel behaved well, in his opinion, which was to say that she followed his advice, engaged those whom he wished to engage, spent money as he directed, and didn't argue with him.

Here in the gardens he could find the only peace possible for him. It wasn't happiness, or even contentment, but it could be merciful oblivion. Nature didn't change. The trees still needed the same care no matter what.

The same was true of Luca, the huge, shabby dog who had wandered in off the streets and attached himself to Vittorio four years ago, refusing to be dislodged. He had followed his chosen master, without complaint, from the grandeur of the villa to the poverty of the rented house, and today he had followed him back to a small copse of trees, to sit hopefully at the bottom of the ladder at the top of which Vittorio was working.

It was rare for him to make any noise, so, when he gave an excited 'wuff', Vittorio looked down.

'What is it?' he asked, seeing nothing.

'Wuff!' Luca repeated, his eyes fixed on the distance.

Then Vittorio understood. Walking towards them was Angel, wearing a colourful silk top and snowy white trousers.

'Stay!' Vittorio ordered hastily.

He was too late. Luca was already bounding away towards her. Vittorio scrambled down the ladder and began to run, but Luca was too fast for him, hurling himself at her, leaving dirty paw marks over the white trousers and clawing the silk blouse until it tore. Vittorio arrived just in time to witness the demolition job.

'I'm sorry,' he said, almost choking on the words.

'Oh, forget it,' she said. 'He's only being friendly.'

Astonished, he realised that she was laughing. Nor had she made any attempt to fend off her new friend, but had dropped down beside him, wrapping her arms about him.

'That's very generous of you,' he said reluctantly. 'But have you seen the state he's left you in?'

She looked down at her clothes and sighed.

'Well, it's a pity, but he didn't mean to. Did you, pet?'

She caressed him again and he nuzzled her, sure of his forgiveness. She stood up, brushing herself down, but with little effect, then wandered over to a fallen tree trunk and used it as a seat.

'Naturally, I shall pay for the damage,' Vittorio said stiffly, although he was wondering how he could afford to replace garments that, for all their apparent simplicity, shrieked expense.

She gave a cheerful shrug. 'I shouldn't bother. He'll only do it again next time.'

'There won't be a next time. I shall keep him away from you in future.'

'Oh, no, don't do that. I love dogs.'

He strolled over and also sat on the tree trunk, taking care to keep a distance from her.

'Yet you don't have one of your own,' he observed.

She made a face which disconcerted him, it made her look so much like a small child.

'I always wanted to have one, but my husband didn't like them.'

Irony overcame Vittorio's manners. 'But surely your husband showered you with every luxury?'

Angel regarded him satirically. 'You've been reading those shallow celebrity magazines. You shouldn't do it. It's a bad habit, and they never tell the truth.'

A point to her, Vittorio thought, annoyed with himself. But he couldn't stay angry. Luca had reared up on his hind legs, draping himself all over Angel again, and she was crowing with delight, tilting her head back so that she seemed to be laughing straight up to the sun. Sunlight poured over her, making her a part of the bright day, giving him a strange, unsettled feeling, as though he was excluded from something wonderful.

'So,' he said lightly, 'he didn't shower you with every luxury?'

'Oh, yes. Every *luxury*. If I wanted diamonds, I had only to ask, but when I set my heart on a nice, big slobbery dog to have fun with, he vetoed it. The mere idea of my expensively elegant person being pawed at made him shudder.'

The satirical way she spoke of 'my expensively elegant person' took Vittorio aback. To hear her making fun of her own reputation was the last thing he'd expected. He wished she wouldn't confuse him.

All he could think of to say was, 'Hmm!' which was a compromise, indicating that his prejudices wouldn't be that easily abandoned.

'Nobody really knows what Joe's like,' she said, interpreting his tone without trouble. 'He wants what he wants and he'll pay for it. But when you cease to please, that's it. The shutters come down and he simply moves on to the next thing. He can be pretty nasty.'

'Is that why you left him?'

'I didn't leave him. He left me. For a younger woman.'

That Vittorio simply didn't believe. His glance at her slender figure and lovely face was full of involuntary admiration that he would have suppressed if he could, but it was beyond his power.

'Younger woman,' he growled. 'What are you? Twenty-two? Three?'

'You underestimate the power of the beauty salon,' Angel said, with a hint of teasing. 'If you've really been reading those magazines you'll know that I'm an artificial construct who owes everything to a silent army, working night and day to conceal the fact that I'm falling to bits. Twenty-two, my foot! I'm a crumbling hag of twenty-eight. Every day pieces of me fall off and have to be fixed back on with safety pins.'

'All right,' he said in a harassed tone. 'I get the idea.'

'I'll bet you don't, not really,' she said, enjoying the joke too much to let it go. 'When I get undressed for bed I take off my wig, remove my nails, and count my fingers to see if any have gone missing. Whatever is left collapses.'

He felt a surge of anger against her. She meant to tease him with that picture of decrepitude, but what had really hit him like a blow in the stomach was 'get undressed for bed'.

Was she mad to talk like that to a man with all his senses about him? Could she really be so unaware of her own power as to risk putting such thoughts into his head? Or didn't it matter, because she saw him only as a servant, and therefore a kind of eunuch?

Whatever the answer, the thought of her stripping off her clothes was one he knew he couldn't afford to indulge for more than a moment. The idea of her in bed was forbidden even for that little moment.

To silence her, Vittorio said coldly, 'Have you finished?'

'Quite finished. I just wanted you to understand that I'm last year's model, so Joe swapped me for one of twenty.'

Angel hadn't mean to confide so much of her personal history, but the sight of Vittorio uneasily trying to decide what to believe was giving her a lot of pleasure. That would teach him to jump to conclusions.

'But—he bought this place for you,' Vittorio said at last. 'All the time I was showing him around he kept saying, "My lady will love this", as though he really cared.'

'But I wasn't his lady by then. She was. He didn't buy this for me, but for *her*. Only she didn't want it. Not grand enough. So he decided that it would "do" for me. He was determined to divorce me as cheaply as possible, and the battle was wearing me out, so I accepted, just to get rid of him.'

If he'd had any doubts about her, they were dispelled by her last words that so closely echoed his own experience with Joe Clannan.

'So you didn't really want to come here?' he asked slowly.

'I was happy enough. I love Italy. I even learned the language once.'

'That surprises me,' he admitted. 'I thought—well—'

'You don't have to say it.' She'd been speaking Italian, but now she added in English, 'You were expecting a miserable old trout.'

'Trout? Excuse me—my English—surely a trout is a fish?'

'Yes, but in England it's also a term of abuse, especially for a woman. I think you had some very bad ideas about me.'

He shrugged, embarrassed. 'I never thought you a—a trout,' he assured her. Then, to get off the awkward subject, he reverted to Italian and asked, 'Do you still want a dog?'

'If you can find me one like him,' she said, indicating Luca, who was shoving his nose against her.

'You've made a bad choice,' Vittorio grunted. 'He's a villain.'

'I can tell. That's why I like him so much.'

'I'll get you one of his offspring. It won't be hard. He populates the district with them. Now, if you'll forgive me, I've taken too much time away from the work you're paying me to do.'

Angel would have laughed and passed it off, but the words were clearly meant to put an end to the brief moment of warmth. She had no choice but to accept her dismissal, and walk away.

For three days Vittorio didn't mention the dog, and Angel thought he had forgotten about it. But on the fourth day he turned up with an animal that looked about four months old and had a marked resemblance to Luca, being brown, untidy, and with mischief in his eyes.

'His name's Toni,' Vittorio said. 'I found a home for him two months ago, but his owner was glad to give him back. Apparently he's noisy, disobedient, uncontrollable, and generally possessed by the devil.'

Angel opened her arms. 'Just what I wanted!' she said eagerly.

He gave a faint grin. 'Don't say I didn't warn you.'

Watching them nuzzle each other, Vittorio could see that it was love at first sight, on both sides.

Angel immediately got him to drive her into Amalfi to buy the cheapest possible jeans and cotton tops and after that she wore nothing else when Toni was around, which was all the time.

She also abandoned make-up, since there was

little point in putting it on when Toni would immediately shove his wet nose against her face. She knew she should reprove him and fend him off, but somehow she never got around to it.

Her truce with Vittorio held, with the 'armed' element becoming less obvious. Angel was wryly aware that she was beginning to win his approval, and even more wryly aware that his approval was worth having.

She practised her Italian on him, as she did with Berta, and was soon talking easily. Then, to tease him, she insisted on having their conversations in English. Vittorio spoke her language well enough to get by, but no more than that, and she told him firmly that it was time he improved. His cynical expression showed that he wasn't fooled, but he let her instruct him, and didn't seem to mind her teasing.

He began to teach her the finer points of lemon growing. She learned that the estate produced the type known as Lisbon, that the right compost was crucial and great care should be exercised with watering.

'Flood them at the start, let them almost dry out, then flood them again,' Vittorio explained. 'And you need patience. It can take years from seed to harvest, so your—the orchards here contain trees at several different stages. Some will be ready to harvest this year, some next, some the year after.'

She didn't miss the way he had begun to say 'your orchards' and hastily changed it to 'the orchards'. Now that she was no longer angry with him, Angel found herself alert to his every nuance, and she thought how painful it must be for him to do this. His love for the place seemed overwhelming, making this a sacrifice that must hurt him to the heart, yet which he endured.

She was beginning to realise that a good harvest was vital. The lump sum Joe had paid her, and which had seemed comfortable at the time, was vanishing fast under the demands she was forced to make on it. Her wage bill alone was alarming. She knew she couldn't do without a car, but she put it off, and finally bought herself only a modest vehicle.

The time was coming when she would be forced to make money somehow, and it made her uneasy because none of the ways open to her were appealing. She'd already had an offer to sell the story of her life with Joe, complete with juicy details, but to do that was to return to the old life and the old values, the very ones she was trying to escape.

Angel pushed the thought aside, telling herself that there would be time enough to worry later.

Just now, she wanted to concentrate on Sam, and getting his new home ready for him.

Every morning and evening she called him, seizing on any sign that he was a little more alert, and concealing her disappointment when he didn't know her. Afterwards she would talk to Roy or Frank, his nurses, and they would be reassuring.

'He's been a little better today—truly—we talk of you, and he seems to understand. He just doesn't recognise your voice on the phone, but it'll be different when he sees you.'

'Of course it will,' Angel would say, trying to convince herself. 'Give him my love. Tell him we'll soon be together again.'

Then she would put the phone down and weep.

# CHAPTER FOUR

VITTORIO USUALLY ended a trip to town by collecting his mail. It eased the confusion caused by the fact that he no longer lived in the big house.

'I've got some for you today,' the post mistress said with a smile. 'And also some for her.'

She said 'her' in the significant tone many of the locals used to signify that they were on his side. This time it troubled him.

'It's not her fault she's the new owner,' he said mildly. 'Perhaps we should ease off.'

A guffaw behind him made him turn to see a young man whom, now he thought of it, he'd never much liked. His name was Mario, a ne'er-do-well who drank too much and lived by doing odd jobs, not very well. Vittorio had hired him as a temporary hand at harvest time, and fired him for laziness.

'I guess she's been working her wiles on you,' Mario said now, sounding not quite sober.

'What do you mean?' Vittorio asked in a cold voice that should have warned him.

'Well, we all know what kind of a woman she is. It's in the papers.'

Moving with deliberate care, Vittorio took Mario's ear between his finger and thumb, squeezing it painfully, and eliciting a squeal.

'I'll tell you just once,' he said, almost gently. 'Shut—*up*! Understood?'

A strangulated gasp signified agreement, and Vittorio released him, turning his back at once.

'I'll take my mail now,' he said. Then he walked out of the shop without a glance at Mario, who was still rubbing his ear and regarding him with malevolence.

Sitting in the car afterwards, he took some deep breaths, clenching his hands on the wheel. To calm himself down he checked over the mail. Among the items for Angel was a large brown envelope that had come from England and was falling apart. He laid everything on the seat and started up.

At the villa he walked straight in, going to the room at the back where there was a desk, from which he had once run the estate. As he laid the brown envelope down it suddenly gave up the ghost and split right open, depositing its contents over the floor, and revealing them to be a collection of English magazines. As he picked them up Angel's face blazed out at him.

She was there on the cover of a publication with a ridiculous name, designed to make every man who read it feel like a daredevil. And her pose reinforced the impression, eyes wide, as though meeting a man's gaze, lips touched by a provocative smile. It was practically an invitation to bed.

Then he saw the words beneath.

*How Angel Broke My Heart—by the lover she dumped.*

Vittorio made a sound of distaste, flinging the magazine down and heading for the door. But something made him stop, turn back and, hating himself, retrieve it.

Inside, there were more pictures from Angel's heyday, but there were also amateur snapshots showing her several years back, looking unfinished and barely recognisable as her present self. With her was a handsome young man, presumably her boyfriend.

The headline claimed that this was *'The True Story Of What Really Happened'*, told by Angel's *broken-hearted fiancé.*

What followed was a tragic tale of a young

man's love spurned by a rapacious woman, who callously threw him over for a rich man. Reading it, Vittorio discovered that his English had improved more than he had realised.

I loved her, and I thought she loved me, but she threw me over for the sake of wealth. How could I compete with Joe Clannan's millions? I bear her no ill-will, but, now that she too has been dumped, I hope she has learned the value of a loving heart.

He grimaced with disgust. Then he took a closer look at the man's face. Like a god, he thought. Probably an empty-headed god, but exactly what a young girl would fall for. But she'd dumped him for Joe Clannan, and Vittorio reckoned he didn't have to be clairvoyant to guess why.

He felt suddenly sad.

Angel, coming into the room a few minutes later, found him sitting, staring into space. She stiffened when she saw the magazine.

'I don't admire your choice of reading matter,' she said coldly.

He jumped as though she'd startled him.

'It belongs to you,' he said, speaking with an effort. 'It was with your mail, which I collected with mine.'

'And you felt you had to open it?'

'The envelope split.' In the face of her sceptical look, he held it up, and she nodded.

He watched as she glanced over the story, and saw a bleak weariness settle over her face. It made her look older, almost haggard. At this moment, he thought, nobody would have recognised her as Angel. He found himself moved by a strange instinct to console her.

'You shouldn't let that thing upset you,' he said. 'They probably sought him out and offered him a good price to say whatever they wanted. It's not important.'

'You mean that's the dirty world I live in, so I shouldn't be surprised,' she said, challenging him directly.

At any other time this was exactly what he would have meant, but not now. While he struggled for a tactful answer she added, 'You're quite right. They probably paid him several thousand for that piece of spite. Good luck to him.'

She gave a hard, mirthless little laugh, that hurt Vittorio to listen to. Suddenly he wanted to think well of her, more than anything on earth.

'But he's made it up, hasn't he?' he asked, almost pleading.

'Some of it. I didn't ditch him for Joe. We'd already broken up by then.'

'But when he says you married your husband for his money—'

'Oh, yes,' she said lightly, challenging him with a look. 'That's perfectly true.'

He paled. 'You don't mean that.'

'Why shouldn't I mean it?' she flung at him defiantly. 'You've met my ex-husband. Did you think I married him for love?'

'I guess not,' he said heavily.

'Don't look like that,' she cried, seized by irrational anger. 'It's what you thought of me anyway, isn't it?'

'Please.'

*'Isn't it?'*

'Well—yes, maybe.'

'Oh, you coward,' she said softly. 'You've despised me from the first day. Admit it!'

He stood silent. After a while she gave a contemptuous laugh.

'It was fine as long as you could sneer at me from a distance, wasn't it? But you can't say it to my face.'

'Maybe because I know how much I got wrong. I blamed you because of the way he bought this house, but you told me yourself it wasn't for you.'

'And you believed me?'

'Of course.'

'Maybe you shouldn't. You have only my word for it.'

'I take your word,' he said through gritted teeth.

'And if I tell you that I was a poor innocent who went blindly into marriage without knowing what I was doing, would you believe me?'

'*Is* that what you're saying?'

'I could if I wanted to. I could say anything if I wanted to. How would you know the difference? For the last eight years I've been living in a world where lies and truth don't exist. There's only what will work for the moment. If it'll do you some good, you say it. If it doesn't work, you change it. The only reality is money. Joe Clannan had millions and he wanted to spend them on me. So I let him. Why not? He bought me, I sold me, and I made sure I got a high price. Is that plain enough for you?'

'Stop it,' he said fiercely. 'Why are you doing this?'

'Just trying to restore your sense of reality. You knew all the worst of me by instinct, the first day. You should have stuck with it. It's all true.'

'*All* of it?'

She drew a sharp breath. 'Most of it. Enough to put any decent man off me, if he had any sense.'

'Then why are you here?' he demanded harshly. 'Why didn't you sell this place and use the money to go on living the high life? The money would have run out in the end, but by that time you could have snared another rich husband easily. It's only a question of the right technique and, according to you, you've got that. Or did I misunderstand you?'

'No, you didn't misunderstand me,' she raged. 'Got the right technique? I've got a dozen of them. There's a way to make a fool of almost any man. You just have to find what it is. Some are more of a challenge than others but, in the end, most of them sit up and beg.'

She could see that he hated this. His eyes darkened and his breathing became fast and shallow. He turned away, but she darted in front of him.

'It's not just a question of fluttering your eyelids. That's a corny old trick, although it still works on the dumber ones—and there are plenty of those. It's knowing when to lick your lips, and a particular note you can put in your laughter because that sends shivers up their spines—'

'Shut up!' he raged. 'Don't you dare say another word.'

She looked up into his face, giving her head a little shake so that her hair fell back in ripples.

'Giving me orders, Vittorio?' she asked softly. 'Isn't it supposed to be the other way around?'

A new darkness came over his face. It would have been frightening if she'd been in the mood to be scared. As it was, a thrill went through her, making her whole body tremble with pleasure.

'I could kill you just for saying that,' he said slowly.

She laughed then, recklessly, knowing what she was doing would push him to the edge, knowing also that she wanted to do exactly that.

'And with some men you have to make them angry first,' she said, leaning forward so that her warm breath fanned his face. 'The result is always the same.'

Vittorio gripped her shoulders hard. 'Are you mad to speak to me like that?' he demanded, giving her a little shake.

'Perhaps. Maybe that's how I get my fun. You must admit that I've made my point.'

'What point?' he asked in a dazed voice.

'I said some men are more of a challenge than others. Actually, you were one of the easier ones.'

'If you think you've brought me under your cheap spell, think again,' he grated. 'Do you think I haven't met women like you before? Do you think I don't know what to do with them?'

'No, you've never met one like me before,' Angel told him, eyes fixed on his face. 'And you're right—you have no idea what to do with me.'

That was true, she thought with bitter triumph. For one defenceless moment it was there in his face—everything he wanted, everything he'd told himself was not for him.

He was holding her tight against him now and she could feel the thunder of his heart, telling her that she was driving him to madness. She began to laugh, at him, at herself, at the sensations pulsing through her.

'Stop that!' he said fiercely. 'Stop it or I'll make you.'

'You couldn't make me,' she challenged.

Vittorio's face tightened, and he jerked her so close that their lips almost touched. A thrill of triumph went through her. This man who defended himself against her with such iron control was melting in her hands.

But in the same moment Angel felt the change inside herself. The brilliant exhilaration faded, died, leaving bleakness behind. She wanted to cry out, grasp it while there was still time, but the time was already over, and there was nothing there.

He saw it all happen, saw the exact instant when her eyes emptied. One minute he was grasping her in anger, the next he was almost holding her up.

'Angel,' he whispered. 'Angel what are you trying to do?'

She shook her head. She didn't know. The mood that had swept over her might have happened a thousand years ago.

He released her carefully, half expecting her to fall, but she stepped back and looked at him with the bleakest expression he had ever seen. He couldn't bear to look at her. It was like watching somebody dying, crumbling inside until only the empty shell was left.

'Why do you want me to think badly of you?' he asked.

'You will anyway, whatever I do,' she said sadly. 'It's safer this way. Go on thinking the worst of me, Vittorio. It's probably true.'

She walked out of the room, leaving him stunned.

He tried to tell himself that everything was very simple. She'd just confirmed his worst suspicions. But he couldn't make himself believe it. She'd spoken cruel, bitter words, all aimed at herself. And every one of them had struck him like a cry for help.

But he didn't know how to help her, and suddenly he wanted to smash something.

Once outside, Angel fled across the hall. When Berta came out from the kitchen, suggesting coffee, she thanked her and declined, then fled up to her room, unable to face even the simplest conversation.

When her bedroom door had closed behind her she let the tension drain from her body and almost fell onto the bed. For a long time she didn't move, just stared into the distance, trying to fight the miserable lethargy that was taking her over.

The last time this had happened was on the night of the quiz show, just as she had gone out into the lights. But that had lasted only briefly. This was swamping her.

It had started in the dark days after she had lost her baby, but she had told herself that she was over them now. Then something would happen to show her that she was mistaken.

The air about her was thrumming, and Vittorio seemed to be there with her again, holding her, losing control, coming to the danger point and taking her with him because her rioting desire matched his own.

That was it. That was what had been lying in wait from the beginning, the thing she had refused to face, that wouldn't be denied any longer.

Then something inside her had failed at the crucial moment. But for that…Angel drew a long breath. *Don't think of it. Don't give him the upper hand.*

She pulled herself together, seizing the magazine

she had grabbed and trying to focus on the words. Gavin seemed to come from another life, and the handsome, stupid face on the page brought back no memories. The more recent picture showed her that he still bore traces of good looks, although growing beefy.

I didn't dump him for Joe, she thought indignantly. I dumped him because he didn't want Sam. He hasn't even mentioned Sam in that piece. Not that I'd want him to.

Toni, who'd slipped into the room behind her, began to clamour for attention.

'OK, let's go for a walk,' she said.

It was an aimless walk, but they both liked it that way. There was something comforting in the company of a creature who didn't expect her to be always striking attitudes. Whatever she wanted to do was fine by him, whether it was wandering, lying down under some trees, or dozing off. When he found her motionless and breathing steadily, he simply curled up in the crook of her arm and stayed with her as the hours passed and the light faded.

Berta was just sitting down for a coffee when Vittorio dropped in late that evening.

'Come and have one,' she called, fetching him a cup. 'In fact, have some supper. There's plenty to spare.'

He accepted gratefully, eating in silence until he had the energy to say, 'That's better. I wasn't looking forward to going home and feeding myself.'

'No, you've been spoilt,' Berta said, with the frankness of long service.

'Spoilt by you,' he agreed. 'I just looked in to give our mistress a report of some of the things that need doing, and how much it's going to cost her to do them.'

'She's not home,' Berta said. 'She went out with Toni hours ago and neither of them have come back. I thought she might have gone to town but her car's here.'

'But it's dark,' Vittorio said, with a worried glance out of the window. 'Has she been out there all this time?'

'Don't tell me you're concerned for her,' Berta said. 'I thought you hated her.'

'I don't hate her,' Vittorio said awkwardly, adding, as though explaining a weakness, 'She's good to the dogs, no matter what they do.' He gave a faint grin. 'She even bought cheap clothes so that they could make a mess of them.'

'Yes, I saw. And she doesn't look the same any more. She's not what we thought.' When Vittorio didn't answer, she said insistently, '*Is* she?'

'I'm not sure,' he mused, remembering what had happened only a few hours ago.

'Did I tell you, she knows all about those murals? When I showed them to her she kept saying, "Ah! That one was painted by…"'

'And was she right?'

'What do I know about pictures? But she knows. And she's speaking Italian better and better after just a week or so. She must have learned it in the past. I wonder why. Just as I wonder why she's doing up those rooms.'

'Which rooms?'

'The ones at the end. That big one and two smaller ones. She's putting beds in them all.'

'Beds? Downstairs?'

'She's having them brought down from upstairs, and the rooms are being spring-cleaned.'

'But what does she say about it?'

'Just that she has some friends coming. She has her own ways of doing things. She's the *padrona*. I can't make her tell me if she doesn't want to. Perhaps she'll tell *you*.'

'I wouldn't dream of asking.'

'Perhaps she's bringing her glamorous friends. They'll have an orgy and it'll be in all the glossy magazines.'

'You should be ashamed of yourself, a respectable woman, talking like that,' Vittorio said severely. 'What do you know about orgies?'

'Only what I've read,' Berta sighed regretfully.

'But I know they drink a lot at them, so perhaps I should ask her about getting in some more wine.'

'You'll do no such thing. Anyway, it wouldn't be in *all* the glossy magazines. It would only be in one, an exclusive, and they'd pay for it. That's how it's done in her world. Sell it for the highest price. Just let her try that here. Just let her try it!'

'You couldn't stop her,' Berta said gently.

He grimaced. 'That's true. And it's time I went to look for her. Whatever she's up to, I can't leave her wandering around in a place she doesn't know. Come on, Luca.'

Together they went out into the darkness.

He wondered if he'd taken leave of his senses. This morning he'd attacked the young oaf in the shop for daring to refer to her reputation. But an hour later she'd been with him, shamelessly flaunting herself, a tease, leading a man on, deserving everything she got.

That was what the world would say, and that cynical, easy judgement would have been his own if he hadn't felt her collapse and seen the light fade and die in her eyes. He knew that he had to find out what was hurting her inside, and until he did he wouldn't know what to think of her.

Yes, he'd taken leave of his senses.

With no idea which direction to take, the man

followed the dog, who seemed sure of himself. After half an hour walking, aided by moonlight, he thought he heard noises from the trees just ahead.

'Hey!' he called again. 'Where are you?'

For answer, he received a squeak, and the next moment Toni came scampering towards him. Vittorio fondled him with relief.

'So where is she?' he asked. 'Go on. I'll follow.'

He had to move fast before Toni vanished into the shadows, but, by following the grunts, Vittorio finally located Angel, sitting on the ground beneath a tree, her arms crossed over her body, rocking back and forth.

'What are you doing out here?' he asked, dropping to his knees beside her.

Her only answer was a little gasp. Looking closely in the gloom, Vittorio saw that her eyes were closed.

'Come on,' he said, taking hold of her.

'Go away,' she whispered.

'I'm not going to go away and leave you here,' he said. 'It's not safe for you to be out alone. What's happened to you? Earlier today you were ready to tell the world to go to hell, especially me.'

'It's all an act,' she said wanly. 'I can't make it last.'

'Angel—'

'Don't!' she said harshly. 'Don't call me Angel. She doesn't exist.'

'I thought that's who you were.'

'No, it's who I pretended to be for eight years. My name is Angela, and that's who I am. At least—I think I am—I don't know—I've been Angel for so long…'

She fell silent, except for the harsh sound of her breathing, and Vittorio slipped his arms about her.

'Come back to the house,' he said gently. 'It's getting cold.'

But she didn't seem to know that he was there.

'I hate Angel,' she said, still in the same gasping whisper. 'She's shallow and stupid and she knows nothing except how things look, and the right thing to say and wear, and what jewellery costs the most, and—'

'Hey, steady, steady,' he said, drawing her closer. 'Why are you suddenly talking like this? Is it because of that nonsense in the magazine? How can you let it worry you?'

'Because it drags me back,' she said in despair. 'I thought I could get free, but I can't. There's no way out because it changes you into someone else—someone you don't want to be.'

He held her, feeling her trembling in his arms,

cursing his own helplessness. He couldn't cope with this. The woman that he knew infuriated him, kept him awake at night wondering, made him want to yell his frustration to the heavens. But when she collapsed into this vulnerable creature it devastated him, and all he wanted was to see her restored. It made no sense at all, and that scared him.

'You've got to stop this,' he urged. 'It isn't you.'

'What is me? Do you know?' Angel had a small flash of anger. 'You're another one who thinks he knows what I'm really like. To blazes with you. To blazes with all of them!'

'That's better,' he said. 'Fight me. Tell me I'm a pain in the neck. You know that's what you really think.'

'Yes,' she said shakily.

'And that's what I've been ever since you came?'

'That's true.'

'And I'm going to go on being just that.'

'Stop it,' she said, thumping him lightly. 'I can't take this. I just need to go and—and—'

'What you need to do is hit me properly, which is what you've been longing to do from the start. It's easy. Go on.'

She did as he said, thumping his shoulder harder and then harder as he urged her on.

'You can do better than that. Remind yourself how much you hate me.'

'No, it's you who hates me,' she said, laughing and crying together. 'Because I'm a spoilt, rich bitch who took your home. You surely remember?'

'I'm not sure I do,' Vittorio said wryly. '*Are* you a spoilt bitch?'

'Didn't I prove it today?'

'Oh, that,' he said, casting his mind back to an incident that felt like a hundred years ago. 'Is that what you were trying to prove? You don't do it very well. I don't think being a vamp comes naturally to you.'

'Oh, hell! I'm sorry, it's just that you—no, it's not your fault. It's me—Angel—one of us. She really is selfish and horrible. You read what Gavin said.'

'Don't tell me this is about that oaf?'

'Not him—everything. Gavin, and Joe, and Sam and—everything.'

'Who's Sam?' he asked, not sure he'd heard her properly.

But Angel was weeping again as the dark waves chased through her mind, and Vittorio gave up talking, just held her tight.

At last he drew away from her, and looked at her face in the faint light from the moon.

'You're a mess,' he said gently. 'Come on, I'm taking you home.'

She choked slightly. 'Not yet. I don't want—'

'I said I'm taking you home,' he said firmly. 'Don't argue.'

She let him draw her to her feet and slip his arm about her waist. They walked in silence until the house was in sight, and she said, in a more normal voice, 'I'm all right now. I don't want anyone knowing about—anything.'

'Don't worry,' he said, releasing her. 'I won't say a word. You can trust me.'

She nodded. 'I know I can.'

They entered the house separately. Angel talked normally to Berta, almost as if her black mood had passed, but Vittorio watched, wondering. After a while, he went out to his battered old car, where he sat for a while, looking up at the window of her room, the room that had once been his own, but which now seemed strange and mysterious to him because she was there.

But no light appeared, and at last he drove away.

Standing at her window in the darkness, Angel watched Vittorio's headlights gradually fading. Then she went to bed, fell asleep at once, and lay undisturbed all night. When she awoke in the morning, the sun was shining and she felt well and strong again.

# CHAPTER FIVE

IT WAS SEVERAL DAYS before Angel saw him again. She was used to him dropping in during the evening, ostensibly for a friendly chat with Berta, but always having a word with her before he left. Gradually she'd come to look forward to these chats, which took the form of more or less friendly bickering, with an exciting edge.

But suddenly Vittorio vanished. She told herself he was just busy, but once, after a trip to Amalfi, she returned to find some estimates of necessary expenditure on her desk. Berta explained that he'd left them there while she was out.

It might have been an accident, but Angel had noticed him as she had driven past him, and could have sworn that he'd seen her. Which meant he'd come to the house when he had known she wasn't there.

Taking the papers, she went out to find him, where he was working in the lemon orchard.

'Do we really need to replace so much of the cliff railing?' she asked. 'You dealt with the place where I fell.'

'Yes, and since then I've had a much closer look at the rest. It's old, and money needs to be spent on it. I'd been planning it next year, but it's worse than I thought, and the work needs to be done before winter. With your permission, I'll put it in hand.'

'Yes, please do that,' Angel sighed.

She would have liked to stay and chat, perhaps even to tell him how his kindness had helped to chase away her demons. But his manner was that of a man impatient to get back to work, and it was as though the word *padrona* was raised like a barrier between them.

Angel understood. He was telling her that they were still mistress and servant, and the events of the other day must be forgotten. He would not presume on them, but—equally important—neither must she.

With a sigh, she turned away. When she looked back a few moments later, Vittorio was absorbed in his work, his head bent. She might not have existed.

As she returned to the house a decision was forming in her head. The thoughts had been hovering for a while as the bills mounted up remorselessly. When the fertiliser had been paid for, a machine would break down and either had to be repaired or bought new. Now she could no longer avoid facing the truth.

After hesitating a little longer, Angel picked up the phone and dialled a London number. It was the direct line to the editor of *GlamChick*.

'Mack?' she said brightly when he came on the line. 'I'll bet you never thought you'd hear from me.'

'My pet, I knew you'd call. You never could resist a good deal, and I offered you a great deal.'

'Oh, you think so? You want to invade my home and pay me peanuts?'

'Invade your home, nothing! We'll do a really high-class photo shoot, showing you in beautiful Italian surroundings, dressed to kill. You talk about your new life, how happy you are, how Joe Clannan can go soak his head because you've found something much better. It'll be a couple of days' work and you'll pocket a nice fat fee.'

'Not quite fat enough, I'm afraid,' she said, trying to sound casual, although her heart was thumping. The next few minutes would be crucial.

'Oho, you want more! OK, I'll play—up to a point. How much more?'

'Double what you offered.'

'Are you out of your mind? *Double?*'

'I think it's worth it for an exclusive.'

'It had better be an exclusive for that price. And there's got to be something new that you never talked about before.'

'It's a deal, then?'

He groaned. 'I suppose it's a deal. But I want it as soon as possible.'

'Then you'd better get a contract out to me quickly.'

'You can't trust my word?'

'I prefer it in black and white.'

'OK. I can see you weren't married to Joe Clannan for nothing.'

Angel laughed. At one time the words might have hurt. Now she was just relieved at having achieved the vital boost to her income.

The contract arrived overnight and she turned it around at once. Two days later, Mack called to say, 'OK, I'm doing this one myself, and I'll leave tomorrow, with a camera crew. There'll be three of us.'

There would just be time to do this before Sam arrived, Angel reflected. In the meantime, they could have the three downstairs rooms that were already prepared.

Angel explained to Berta that their guests would be from a magazine. There was no point in hiding the truth.

Berta merely said, 'Yes, *padrona*. I will arrange food and wine.'

But Angel could sense her surprise and disapproval. No doubt she would call Vittorio's mobile phone as soon as possible. Angel had confirmation of that when he arrived at the house later that day on some trivial piece of business that could have waited. He didn't mention what he knew, but he looked at her in a way that there was no mistaking.

It hurt after their brief moment of closeness. His expression contained as much sadness as cynicism, saying that he'd been right about her all the time.

She could have said, Look, I need the money to pay all those bills you keep presenting me with. Then given him chapter and verse on just how meagre Joe's settlement had been.

But her temper flared into life, telling her that pigs would fly before she explained herself to him. After snubbing her for days, who the hell did he think he was to judge her so easily?

'Don't let me keep you,' Angel said coolly, and saw his face harden against her.

She knew her temper boiled over too easily these days. Eight years of keeping it strictly under control had left her glad of the release of anger. As Vittorio walked away there was even a bitter satisfaction in knowing that she had the upper hand.

She repented almost at once.

'I'm not a nice person,' she muttered. 'What's happening to me?'

But it was too late to call him back, and her mind was becoming filled with darkness and tension again.

'Not again,' she whispered. 'Please, not again. Not until this is over.'

It was hard to resist the thought that this had happened because Vittorio had turned against her, but she told herself not to be absurd. The mere idea that the offer or withdrawal of his friendship could affect her like this was one that she wouldn't tolerate.

On the afternoon before Mack and the photographers were due to arrive, Vittorio said, 'Do you want me to meet your friends at the airport?'

'No, thank you. That isn't your job. I've made arrangements.'

'Yes, *padrona*,' he said politely, and left.

A hired car and chauffeur would be waiting for them at Naples airport. Angel had chosen not to go there herself, because she wanted to spend all the time on her appearance. It took an hour to decide on the dress. The one she finally chose was white and luxuriously simple, with a V-neckline that plunged down between her breasts, suggesting, but not quite revealing.

Her face took even longer. She'd never depended on make-up artists, but she'd learned from them and could now produce the desired effect unaided: just enough darkening around her large eyes to make them even more emphatic, the luscious gleam added to her lips.

Then her hair, shining, tumbling over her shoulders, long enough to flick this way and that in tempting attitudes. She'd wondered if she'd forgotten how to do all these things, but the skills returned to her with disturbing ease.

She was downstairs an hour before they were due, checking and re-checking the bedrooms, the kitchen where Berta was preparing a feast, the dining room where the table was laid with crystal and silver. She declared everything perfect, which made Berta beam.

Vittorio appeared, carrying a heavy silver dish, and it suddenly struck her as odd that he should be here. Odder still was the fact that he was smartly dressed in black trousers and snowy white shirt, with a dark red bow tie. With a sense of outrage, Angel realised what he looked like.

'Why are you dressed like a waiter?' she demanded.

'I suppose that's what I am,' he said mildly.

'I've offered to help Berta serve the meal. We want to make the best impression on your friends, *padrona*.'

That last remark sounded like a calculated insult, she thought. She knew why he'd done this—not to be helpful, but to stay here and make his disapproval obvious. With difficulty, Angel restrained her temper and said calmly, 'That's very obliging of you.'

Vittorio nodded like a good servant, set the silver dish down and left the room. But she followed him into the hall, seized his arm and forced him to turn.

'Just what do you think you're doing?' she flashed.

'Being obliging, *padrona*.'

'The hell you are! You fixed this so that you could keep me under your eye. How dare you spy on me?'

His eyes narrowed and she guessed he wasn't used to being spoken to like that. But it was his own fault for provoking her.

'Why are you so determined to think the worst of me, *padrona*?'

'Don't call me that! Do you hear? Don't ever do it again.'

'But it's the truth. We are mistress and servant. If I can face it, why can't you?'

'The way you say it, it's a sick joke.'

His eyes raked over her, and she understood the implication. It *was* a sick joke.

'How dare you?' she breathed.

'What do you want me to say? The other night you rejected Angel. You said she was shallow and stupid and knew nothing except how things seemed on the surface. There was an honest woman talking, a true woman, with a heart. But now? Look at you. You've turned into that creature again and invited the world in to see you using my home as a backdrop to your shallowness. And I say that by doing so you desecrate it. There now, are you answered?'

Vittorio was sorry as soon as the words were out of his mouth. The gaze Angel turned on him was stricken, as though he'd struck her a savage blow. He hadn't meant to. Lashing out defensively, he'd forgotten the vulnerability she strove so hard to conceal, but he could see it now in the dark shadows in her eyes, so like the ones he'd seen before.

'Look,' he said hastily, 'take no notice—'

But before he could finish there was a sound from outside, and a man's voice called, 'Angel, where are you?'

Instantly Vittorio saw something come over her. She straightened up, adjusted her shoulders, and took a deep breath. Then, right there in front of him, she turned into someone else. Her eyes grew brighter, her mouth stretched into a calculated, dazzling smile. She was Angel again.

Then she was hurrying towards the front door, arms outstretched to meet the three men descending from the car. The first one, a great bear of a man, enveloped her in a hug, bawling, 'Angel, my sweet!'

'Mack, *darling*!'

Vittorio watched her embrace each of the three men one by one, laughing, teasing them, apparently overwhelmed with delight. If he hadn't seen the transformation a moment ago, he would have believed every word of it. Now he could only see the strain behind each word and gesture.

He heard the beefy man say, 'You really made them pay over the odds for this, so let's make it a good one.'

Then Angel's tinkling laugh, and the provocative words, 'Well, a man ought to pay over the odds, and I always give good value.'

Mack gave a lecherous guffaw that made Vittorio want to knock him to the floor.

He wondered what she would say if she knew that he had volunteered to help out today, not to spy on her, but simply to be there if she needed him. She would probably laugh, he thought, exasperated with himself. It drove him wild that his hostility was constantly undermined by a mysterious urge to protect her.

When everyone had been installed in their rooms, there was wine and cakes. Then Angel began to show them around while the photographers inspected the house, seeking angles, setting up lights. Vittorio kept severely away from them.

Then the pictures began: Angel in the garden, flooded with bright sunlight, walking through the roses by the fountain, Angel the expert lemon-grower, indicating the terraces. From a high-up window in the house, Vittorio watched this at a distance.

When they returned they were still discussing lemons, and Mack was saying admiringly, 'You've really become an expert in a short time.'

'It's not down to me,' Angel disclaimed quickly. Seeing Vittorio crossing the hall, she said, 'This is the real expert. I only know what Vittorio teaches me.'

'Is that so?' Mack said, advancing on Vittorio in a friendly spirit. 'So, you're the guy that Angel relies on?'

Vittorio gazed at him blankly. *'Scusi?'*

'Angel says you know all about lemons.'

Mack spoke slowly, but it didn't seem to help. Vittorio simply stared. After a moment he said in a carefully stupid voice, 'Me no spikka da English.'

'Cut that out,' Angel muttered, half annoyed, half amused. 'You "spikka da English" perfectly well when it suits you.'

Vittorio reverted to Italian to say, 'But in the presence of your eminent friends my wits desert me. I am overwhelmed to meet such great people—'

'Shut up!' she said, trying to fight back her laughter. 'Don't play games with me or I'll stamp on your foot.'

He grinned. '*Scusi, signora.* Me no spikka da English.'

'Get lost.'

'*Si, signora.*' He gave her the grin of a conspirator and glided away before she could reply.

'Angel, honey, can we have you over here?'

Angel sashayed back, giving Mack a wink and twisting her hips in a way that had the photographers begging for more. She felt strong and ready for anything. It made no sense that Vittorio could do this merely by grinning and sharing a joke with her, but then a lot about her response to this man didn't make sense.

For dinner she changed into a black, figure-hugging evening gown, and descended slowly, stopping to pose every few steps. When Mack gallantly offered her his arm, she caught a look of faint surprise on his face.

'I forgot, you've seen this one before, haven't you?'

'I admit I thought you'd have raided the couture establishments in Milan and Rome by now.'

'At one time I would have done, but these days I'm just a simple country girl.'

'That's going to come as a great disappointment to your male admirers.'

'There, and I thought it was me they loved, and not the trappings.'

Laughing, they went into the dining room, where Angel posed for more pictures as the perfect hostess of a sumptuous feast. Mack sat next to her, mentally taking notes, she was sure. He'd been interviewing her on and off all day, but she knew that the serious business was still to come. For what the magazine was paying, he'd made it clear he would expect more than platitudes.

Somewhere in the background she heard the house phone ring. After a moment, Vittorio came to find her.

'There's a man on the phone for you, *padrona*.'

'Did you ask his name?'

'No, *padrona*,' he said quietly.

Puzzled, Angel went into the hall and took up

the receiver. The called turned out to be Roy, one of Sam's carers.

'Sam asked me to call you right now,' he said. 'He's feeling bright and on top of things.'

'Wonderful!'

Then Sam's voice, saying, 'Hello, darling. How's my girl?'

'Sam,' she said eagerly. 'Oh, it's wonderful to hear you. I miss you so much.'

'I miss you too, darling. How do you like Italy?'

He even remembered that she was in Italy. The pleasure of finding his mind so clear made Angel laugh aloud.

'It's lovely here,' she said. 'But it'll be even nicer when you're here too.'

'When am I coming?'

'Not long now, darling, we'll soon be together again.'

Vittorio, carrying things from the kitchen to the dining room, tried not to overhear, but the words seemed to stab him.

Mack was buzzing with eagerness when she returned.

'Come on, tell. Who's the man phoning you? A new lover? I thought you'd have been followed by hordes of lustful Italians by now. Can I tell my readers how you like Italian men?'

She gave a teasing laugh. 'Mack, I promise you, Italian men are just like men the world over.' She leaned close and whispered, 'Very, very annoying.'

He chuckled, and the dangerous moment passed, but soon she knew she would have to confront the question of exactly how much she would tell him. How much could she *bear* to tell him?

Then she thought of the estate, peaceful and beautiful beneath the noonday sun. She thought of the lemons, gently ripening, ready for their moment of splendour when they would rescue the whole estate. She thought of the people who depended on her: Berta, the maids, the gardeners. She thought of Vittorio, bitter and awkward, but working selflessly to save the place he loved.

And she knew what she was going to say.

After dinner Angel took Mack into a small side room, which had once been used as a library, although most of the books had gone.

'Let's talk about Joe,' he said. 'How did you feel when he told you he'd found someone else?'

Angel managed a shrug. 'Not really surprised. We'd been drifting apart for some time.'

'Had you found another man?'

'No, I never played around, so stop looking hopeful,' she said with a hint of teasing.

'Not one lover, hovering in the background?'

'Not one. Give up.'

He gave a resigned sigh, and she thought she'd won this round, but he was preparing his bomb-shell.

'Have you heard anything about Joe and Merry's wedding?' he asked with a casual air.

'No, but our divorce became final last week, so I guess it'll be soon.'

Mack grinned, reaching into a leather bag he was carrying, and whipping out a bunch of photos that he spread over the table in front of her. They showed a wedding. Joe Clannan grinned fatuously at his young bride, who resembled an overgrown meringue adorned with too much satin, too much lace, and too many diamonds.

'They married two days ago,' Mack said, watching her face closely. 'Didn't you know?'

'Why should I know? I don't think they planned to invite me. Good luck to them.'

'You can say that, even now you've seen what she's wearing around her neck?'

Angel shrugged, trying to seem light-hearted. She'd been hoping Mack wouldn't make the connection.

'Angel, c'mon, this is me, Mack. I did the first ever interview you gave after you married this man eight years ago, and you showed me the necklace he'd just given you. You told me what a pretty speech he made about "his special lady", how he'd dreamed of seeing it about your neck.'

*Tell them a good tale, darling,* Joe had said. *I must have said something charming and romantic, but you fill in the details.*

'Now it's around another woman's neck,' Mack continued remorselessly. 'Don't try to pretend it isn't the same one.'

'OK, it's the same one. Joe wanted it back and I agreed as part of our divorce settlement.'

'Did he leave you with any jewellery at all?' Mack asked shrewdly.

'You don't understand. This is my new life. I don't need all those baubles. He's welcome to them.' She gave a faint, bored yawn. 'To be honest, I was getting rather tired of that life. It looks fun from the outside—clothes, money, jewels, parties—but then you start to realise you're on a treadmill. The same party seems to come round again and again.

'I can remember one night when I got confused and thanked someone for a wonderful evening, thinking she was the hostess. Actually I'd been to a party at her house the previous week. The real hostess was someone I'd been talking to several minutes before, and I have a horrible feeling that I said it was a dull evening.'

Mack laughed and urged her on. 'So the whole life was beginning to pall?'

'Yes, it was. I found I wanted something more, something I was never going to find under the glittering lights.'

'Can you remember when this feeling started?'

Angel took a deep breath. She'd known this moment would come, and now there was no turning back.

'Yes, it started when I lost my baby,' she said simply.

Mack's face showed his amazement. This was one story that had never got out. Mercifully, he had the tact to keep silent while she went on,

'It happened in the third month. I wanted a baby with all my heart, and, when I lost it, I was devastated. Nothing was the same after that. I was a different person and Joe—well, as I say, we began to drift apart.'

Once she'd sworn never to give such an interview, and now it hurt as much as she'd known it would. But it was the only way to earn enough to protect those who relied on her. And, as she went on talking, she had the comforting feeling that she was fighting off enemies, watching them retreat.

Mack pressed for more. He would have liked her to bad-mouth Joe, but she saw what he was up to and shook her head.

'I've already given you a real exclusive,' she said. 'I've filled my part of the bargain.'

'Sure, you've really earned your money, I'll give you that. But Joe doesn't come out of it well—'

'Not through anything I've said,' she interrupted him firmly. 'Now, hush up, Mack, and I'll tell you something else. I didn't want anyone to know that I'd miscarried, so three days later I did a TV show.'

His eyes lit up. 'The show must go on, huh? That was very brave.'

'Not really, because I was living in a trance, and between doing a show, or telling people the reason why not, it was easier to do the show.'

'But didn't your husband—?'

'Mack, it was my decision, nothing to do with Joe. I'm my own woman, you know. Always was, always will be.'

'I reckon there's a lot more to you than meets the eye—oh, thanks, yes, I will have another whisky.'

This last was addressed to Vittorio, hovering like a shadow with the decanter. Angel was startled. She hadn't known he was there.

He refilled Mack's glass before asking,

'Something for you, *signora*?' He leaned closer to her to ask, 'A cup of tea?'

'I'd love a cup of tea,' she said at once, wondering what instinct had led him to the perfect conclusion. It was almost as though he were inside her head.

And as he turned to leave Angel almost thought she felt a comforting hand on her shoulder. But it was so light that she might have imagined it.

When the tea arrived it was just how she liked it, and it gave her the energy to carry on. In the end it was Mack who yawned.

'I was up at four this morning,' he said. 'Can we finish this tomorrow?'

'Sure.'

In the hall she said goodnight to him and the photographers, then returned to the kitchen to thank Berta for the meal.

'And for the tea,' she said. 'It was perfect.'

'As good as the English?' Berta asked slyly.

'Better than the English.' They laughed and Angel looked around. 'Where's Vittorio?'

'He left, *padrona*. But he will be here tomorrow. He said so.'

'That's lovely.'

It was absurd to feel disappointed, but she'd been sure he would wait and talk to her. There was nothing to do but go to bed and lie there in the darkness, feeling lonely, until she fell asleep and her dreams were haunted by the sound of fading footsteps.

# CHAPTER SIX

IN THE MORNING Angel rose, telling herself that this would be over soon. Not long to go now, just a few more hours.

More pictures, outside, by the railings, looking down onto the long drop. She was co-operative, suggesting new poses, making the photo session last as long as possible. As she posed she glanced around for Vittorio, but there was no sign of him. He would be at the house, she told herself.

But, when they returned indoors, he wasn't there.

The cameramen were packing up and there was no way of putting Mack off any longer.

'Let's talk about Gavin Alford.'

'Gavin who?'

'The lad who wrote that tell-all piece about you. Or perhaps you didn't see it?'

'Yes, I saw it, but I promise you there was very little "all" to tell. We were young, we dated, we broke up.'

'Because of Joe's money?'

Angel managed a tinkling laugh. 'Good heavens, no. Gavin was history by then. Not that he was ever anything much. He meant well, but his conversation was rather limited.'

Remembering Gavin's well-paid lies, she reckoned she could allow herself that little bit of revenge.

It was nearly over. Soon she would be free of them.

But Mack had one final shot.

'Your baby—what sort of plans did you have? Had you chosen any names yet?'

Out of sight Angel clenched her hands, but there was no sign of strain in her voice as she spoke. 'I didn't know if it was a boy or a girl and it was too soon to think of names…'

That wasn't true. She'd made lists of names, both male and female, but Joe hadn't been interested. He'd simply refused to discuss their child, either when she had been carrying it or after she'd lost it.

But she wouldn't say that. Instead, she talked around the subject for ten minutes, and Mack seemed satisfied.

At last it was over. They were making moves toward the front door.

But then someone said, 'Hey, did you hear…?'

and they stopped again, prolonging the farewell by a few more excruciating minutes.

'Yes,' Angel heard herself saying. 'Isn't that fascinating? Yes—yes—'

If they didn't go soon she thought she would start to scream.

Then she heard Vittorio's voice, breaking into the inanities.

'Let me help you with your bags, *signore*.'

She hadn't known he was there. It was as though he'd materialised by a miracle. Before anyone could speak, he had picked up two heavy bags and strode out of the front door to place them beside the van. He came back, seized two more and strode out with them. The message was unmistakable: *go!*

Such was the intimidating power of his presence that everyone obeyed him, almost slinking out, as though awed by his authority. Angel followed them out to say more polite farewells, and felt Vittorio's hand under her elbow.

As the door of the van slammed and the crew leaned out of windows, waving, calling, Vittorio murmured in her ear, 'Don't give in now. Just a few more moments, and they'll be gone.'

So he understood. She'd thought he was enraged by their presence, to the point of throwing them out. But now she knew he'd done it for her. The hand under her elbow grew firmer, steadying her, offering strength.

The engine started, the van turned, and then it was moving away from them. It was mercifully over.

'All right?' Vittorio asked quietly.

'I am now.'

He turned her gently and led her back into the house, his arm about her waist. He didn't move it until she was sitting on the sofa, and then he took her hands in his.

'Why do you do this to yourself?' he demanded. 'Why did you tell him all that?'

'You heard?'

'Yes, I was listening. Perhaps it was wrong of me, but now I understand many things about you, so I can't be sorry I did it. But you didn't have to tell him.'

'I did,' she said, turning her hands slightly so that she could clasp his in return. 'You don't know—you don't know—'

'No, I don't know anything about you, do I? I keep thinking I do, but there's always another mystery. Don't keep things to yourself.'

She tried to pull herself together. 'I'm all right—honestly, I'm all right.'

'That is a lie,' he said simply. 'You're breaking apart. You need to talk to a friend. If not me then— someone else.'

'If not you then nobody,' she said huskily. 'Funny isn't it—that you should be the best friend I have?'

'Yes, it's funny,' Vittorio agreed gravely. 'But I suppose it's true.' Suddenly he said, almost violently, 'For pity's sake, don't suffer alone. If I'm your friend then let me *be* a friend. Let me help you. Tell me what to do.'

'Nothing,' she said. 'It's in my head—a kind of darkness. It isn't here all the time—but sometimes—the doctor said it would go, and I keep thinking it has, but then...'

'Is it because you lost your baby?'

'Yes, that's when it started. I fell down into a dark pit. Sometimes I think I see a way out, but it always comes back.'

Vittorio let out a long breath and silently called himself a fool. Then he did the only thing possible and put his arms around her, holding her tightly against him.

'Go on,' he said. 'I want to hear the rest.'

'The rest?'

'The bits you didn't tell Mack.'

'Joe got fed up with me always being depressed,' Angel said at last. 'He said I was no fun any more.' Vittorio swore with soft violence.

'How much fun was a grieving woman supposed to be?'

'He never thought of me as grieving. He hadn't wanted a child and he couldn't understand me being any different. Being fun was my job. He liked to see me teasing other men just enough to get them worked up, but always going home with him.' She gave a self-mocking laugh. 'I got quite good at that.'

'Yes, I remember,' Vittorio said wryly.

'I'm sorry. You just made me mad, and I thought you were just one of them.'

He didn't have to ask what 'one of them' meant.

'In the end he got fed up with me being unhappy and started looking around. It was inevitable that he should find another woman. I didn't care. I was glad to get out of that marriage, even if it meant accepting a mean settlement.'

'Yes, you don't have to tell me that he's a cheapskate. What he did to me, he did to you.'

'I got this place and a lump sum, which seemed plenty at the time, but I had no idea of the things I'd have to pay for. I had to make some money to carry us through until harvest, so I extorted a huge fee out of Mack. But in return—'

'In return you had to bare your soul,' he said softly. 'And I judged you. Forgive me.'

'It's all right. I'll be better now that this is over. In some ways I'm even glad. I've never talked about it before. There was nobody to tell.'

'I wish you'd told me.'

'What, the man who thought I was a wicked witch put on earth to torment him?' Angel said with a jerky little laugh.

'That seems a long time ago. I'm not sure it ever happened.'

'Maybe it didn't,' she agreed.

A feeling of sweetness and contentment was stealing over her. It was something to do with the gentleness of his voice and his touch. At this moment she felt no desire, only a longing to stay here, resting against him, for ever.

As though he'd sensed her thoughts, Vittorio said, 'Promise me something.'

'What?'

'That you won't bear things alone any more. That you will come to me, as a friend, and tell me what you suffer.'

'I promise,' she said softly. 'If I need help, I'll come to you. I seem to have been taking your help ever since I came here. What would I have done if you hadn't stayed?'

'I would always have stayed. You tried to get rid of me, remember?'

'Yes, I didn't understand that you're part of this place. It still belongs to you more than me…'

'Don't say that,' he said harshly, getting to his feet.

'Why not, if I've come to see that it's true—?'

'I said *stop it*!' he shouted. 'Are you really so stupid that—'

He checked himself with a sharp breath. Then he stalked out through the French windows into the garden, leaving Angel calling herself every name she could think of.

By now Angel was familiar with Vittorio's way of retreating whenever they had a moment of closeness, as though scenting danger. So she reckoned she knew what to think when, next morning, Berta met her with the news that he'd called to say that he'd be away a few days, 'exploring new markets for the estate produce'.

He might have spoken to her directly, but he'd sent the message through Berta. So he was avoiding her. And perhaps he was wise. The mood that was growing between them—a combination of emotion and half-admitted desire, spiced with a hostility that still sometimes flared up—left Angel not knowing what to think. It was sweet, intense and fast becoming the most thrilling experience of her life, but her heart was as wary as his.

For a woman of twenty-eight she knew strangely little of love. Once she'd thought herself in love with Gavin, but when she'd seen his true colours she'd dumped him without hesitation and shed few tears.

She'd been fond of Joe for a while, until his behaviour disgusted her. He'd been a selfish lover, demanding extravagant appreciation in return for the least possible effort. The result had been to send her heart and body to sleep. Angel couldn't remember the last time she'd felt anything like desire, and had come to believe that it was something she would never know.

But Vittorio had startled her awake. She was alive again, both in her heart and body, alive in ways she had never known before. He was in her thoughts when he was present, and even more when he was not. If he was there, she loved to contemplate him, so much so that she had to check herself for fear he would suspect. Even so, her eyes and her thoughts would sneak back, uncontrollably, to the source of their delight.

But mingled with the pleasure was dismay.

It would have to be him, she told herself, exasperated. Of all the men that I wouldn't choose—why him? He couldn't be an elegant man of the world, ready to fall at my feet like the others, could he? Oh, no! I had to pick an awkward curmudgeon who's fighting this as hard as I am.

When she found him gone that morning, her thoughts became positively grumpy.

'How did I let this happen? Gee, if I have unluck! Not just bad luck, but *un*luck—like vampires are undead. Why him? That's what I want to know. *Why him?*'

'*Padrona?*'

She discovered that Berta was looking at her in alarm, and realised that she must have spoken aloud. Thank goodness Berta's English was still basic.

The two of them used the next few days to put the downstairs bedrooms in order. Sam and his nurses would be here soon, and now Angel explained everything to Berta, who was sympathetic.

'Poor old man,' she said. 'I cook a special meal for him.'

On the appointed day Angel prepared to drive herself to the airport.

But, when she tried to start up her car for the journey, it died a death.

Berta's face showed what she thought of someone who seriously expected the battered object to complete a long journey, or even to start it. But the next moment she was smiling, pointing, and calling, 'There!'

Looking around, Angel saw, with relief, that Vittorio's car was heading for them.

'Thank goodness,' she gasped, running down the path and waving her arms.

He stopped so sharply that he swerved. Putting his head out, he yelled, 'Have you gone crazy?'

'Yes,' she said, bounding into the seat beside him. 'I need you to take me to the airport. My car's given up and I have to meet Sam. Please hurry. I simply can't be late for him.'

Leaning out of the window to give a thumbs-up to Berta, Angel missed Vittorio's grimace as he swung the car around, and his muttered, 'I see.'

'They should land at eleven-thirty,' she said. 'And I thought I was all right, but I've wasted so much time trying to get that car to start—can't you go any faster?'

'Not on these roads,' he said, jerking his head to indicate their route along the cliffs.

After a while he said, 'How many are we collecting?'

'Three.'

'How are we going to get three people plus luggage into this little car?'

'We won't have to. I've arranged things the same way I did when Mack and the photographers came. A hire firm at the airport is providing a car big enough for them. But this time I want to be there.'

'To meet Sam?'

'That's right.'

She answered casually, but in the silence that followed it dawned on her that Vittorio had spoken with an ironic edge to his voice.

Of course, she thought, he didn't know who Sam was. Was it possible that he actually believed…?

Glancing sideways at his fiercely set face, Angel decided that it was possible. He thought Sam was her lover. And he minded. He might deny it until kingdom come, but she knew with ancient, instinctive wisdom that he was jealous.

Well, he would discover the truth in an hour or so. Until then, she thought cheerfully, let him suffer. Serves him right! She wasn't sure exactly what Vittorio had done to deserve suffering, but she would think of something. For the moment she only knew that the sun shone more brightly and the air was singing.

'I'm sorry if I urged you to go too fast,' she said. 'It's just that I can't wait to be with Sam again. It seems so long since I saw him. We talk every day, but it's not the same.'

'I'm sure.'

Apparently oblivious to the discouragement in his voice, Angel chattered on. 'I've done all I can to make things perfect for him.'

'I'm sure he'll appreciate that.'

'And it'll be wonderful being able to be with

him all the time. In the past—well, things have been difficult.'

'I wonder how your husband felt about him,' Vittorio said grimly.

'Well, he wasn't happy, but he knew that Sam couldn't be dislodged from my life. Can we go a little faster?'

An hour later they were pulling in to Naples airport a few minutes after the plane was due to land. She went first to the car-hire firm to secure their vehicle, then hurried to the exit from the customs area, through which they must come.

'Have we got time for a coffee first?' Vittorio asked.

'You go. I'm going to stand here to catch the first glimpse of him. I don't want to miss one second.'

'Fine, we'll both stay.'

After that Angel seemed to glue herself into position, her eyes fixed eagerly on the people coming through the doors. Watching her, Vittorio realised that she had forgotten him. She had no attention for anyone but the man who was about to arrive and transform her world. The glow in her eyes, her air of vibrant happiness, told its own story.

For the hundredth time Vittorio asked himself why he allowed this woman to make a fool of him.

But this was it. This was the last time. He'd drive her and her paramour home, then he'd vanish from sight. He'd tend the estate and communicate with her at a distance.

'There he is! *There he is!*'

He was roused from his thoughts by Angel's delighted shriek. She was waving at someone who was emerging from Customs. Vittorio saw an extremely handsome young man wave back, smiling straight at her. He waited for Angel to run and throw herself into his arms.

Then Vittorio saw that the young man was not alone. He was accompanied by another man, elderly and frail, who gazed around him as if puzzled.

'It looks like he's brought his grandfather,' Vittorio observed.

'That's not his grandfather,' she breathed. 'It's mine. *Sam!*'

Before his astonished eyes, she darted forward and threw her arms around the old man, while her glad cry of, 'Sam, oh, Sam!' floated back.

Vittorio watched them, feeling the world right itself again, the sun come out and the birds start to sing right there in the airport.

The young man had been joined by another, and the two of them were taking care of a lot of luggage, which seemed to include a wheelchair.

Sam appeared confused, merely patting Angel vaguely and barely returning her greeting. But she seemed oblivious, her delight at seeing him so overwhelming that it blotted out all else. She began to lead him forward, but he looked around for the young men, whose presence evidently reassured him.

'Vittorio,' Angel said, approaching him, 'this is my grandfather. This is Sam.'

Vittorio extended his hand, which the old man took, but vaguely.

'And these are Roy and Frank, his friends.'

She said the last two words carefully, and he understood that these were carers.

Walking slowly, they guided Sam out to the cars.

'I'll take Sam with me,' Angel said.

'It might be better if you don't,' Roy said quickly. 'The journey's left him a bit disorientated.'

'But he's got me now,' she said happily. 'It'll be all right.'

Hugging Sam's arm, she began to draw him to the car, but he looked nervous.

'Who are you?' he asked in a trembling voice. 'Where are you taking me?'

'Home, darling.'

'But I don't know this place.'

'Don't worry,' she said, looking at him fondly. 'I'm here. You'll be all right.'

He stared at her. 'Who are you?'

'I'm Angela, your granddaughter. And I'm taking you home.'

Sam cast a worried look at Frank and Roy, but he didn't argue further, and allowed himself to be led away.

'Tell your driver to follow me,' Vittorio said, and joined them in the car.

Angel got into the back with Sam. She was still happy, but the first edge of her joy had gone. If only he had recognised her, just this one time. But he just needed a little time, she assured herself. She talked brightly, holding his hands between hers, telling him about their new home, asking him questions about how he'd been without her.

Vittorio, listening, was torn with pity for her. He couldn't see her face but he knew from her voice how determinedly she was refusing to recognise the blank nothingness that was coming from the old man.

'I've missed you so much, Sam. It was lovely when you called me the other night.'

'What are you talking about? I never called you.'

'Yes, you did, and we talked about how it

would be when you arrived. You're going to love your new home.'

'Where are we?'

'This is Italy, and we're going to a lovely house, and—'

'I want to go home. Who are you? Why are you making me go with you?' His voice rose higher. 'Let me go.'

He began to struggle with the car door, growing more upset by the moment.

'Sam, *please*—'

'This is dangerous, we've got to stop,' Vittorio said, pulling over onto the hard shoulder, and watching his mirror to see that the other car had stopped behind them. 'Get one of those lads, quick.'

Roy was already running towards them, pulling open Sam's door, taking the old man into his arms.

'Help me,' Sam wept.

'Let me take him with us,' Roy said to Angel. 'He'll calm down.'

'Yes, do what he wants,' she said raggedly.

'Come and sit beside me,' Vittorio urged her, patting the front passenger seat.

'No, thanks, I'll stay back here,' she said bleakly. 'It's not far.'

She wouldn't budge on this, and he was forced

to drive the rest of the way trying to imagine what was happening in the back seat. Was she all right? Was she badly upset? He strained his ears but he could hear nothing.

After a while she said in a normal voice, 'I should have known better than to separate him from the lads. Of course he's confused, after not seeing me for a while, and then the journey—I expected too much. That's all it is. Everything's going to be fine.'

Her determined cheerfulness was more painful to him than tears would have been, but there was no comfort he could offer, and he could only say, 'Of course it is.'

After that she didn't speak again for the rest of the journey.

# CHAPTER SEVEN

VITTORIO ATE in the kitchen that evening, waiting until the house was quiet. He would have given a great deal to know what was happening, but although he could hear the others moving about it was impossible to guess details.

Berta, who served their meal, was cheerful because Sam seemed to have a hearty appetite. 'He's gone to bed,' she told Vittorio when she'd collected the coffee cups. 'One of the nurses has gone too, and the other one is talking to the *padrona*. I think she's upset.'

Later she took them more coffee and returned with the information that the other nurse had retired for the night. Vittorio lingered awhile, then strolled out into the garden, where he could see Sam's darkened windows.

As he'd half hoped, Angel was there, sitting on the sloping lawn that led down from the terrace, looking up at the rising moon, and the stars that were just beginning to appear in the softly darkening sky.

'So that's Sam?' he observed, dropping down beside her.

'Yes, that's my darling Sam.'

'Did it get any better after he arrived?'

'Not really,' she said despondently. 'He's all right when he's with the boys, but he doesn't know me.'

'How long has he been this way?'

'About nine years, maybe a little more. He's not always like today. Like I said, I handled it badly.'

That was probably true, yet it hurt him to hear her finding reasons to blame herself. He risked saying gently, 'Is he ever very much better than today?'

'Oh, yes, he often knows who I am.'

'And he often doesn't,' Vittorio said shrewdly. 'That must be hard for you.'

'Yes,' she said a little huskily. 'But I know he's all right with Roy and Frank.'

'It must cost you a fortune to pay their salaries, and I expect there are other expenses.'

'Yes, the extras add up. But I don't want Sam to go without anything he needs. He never let me go without.'

'Is this where Joe came into the equation?'

Angel nodded. 'I told you I married him for his

money. It was a fair bargain. I got what I wanted for Sam, Joe got a trophy wife to flaunt. I did all I promised him, jumped through every hoop he wanted, acted sexy, gazed at him adoringly. It was quite an act but, if I say it myself, I put on a good show, because I keep my word.'

'For pity's sake, you don't have to justify yourself to me.'

She looked at him quizzically and he had the grace to blush.

'I supposed I deserved that,' he grunted.

'I didn't say anything.'

'You didn't have to. From the first day I acted as though you owed me explanations. I judged you in ignorance, and—'

'Hey, that's enough,' she said, reaching over and taking his hand. 'We've put all that behind us.'

'So I thought, but I keep learning new things about you, and discovering again how wrong I was.'

'It's all right,' she said, squeezing his hand tightly. 'Friends.'

Angel thought Vittorio hesitated a long time before agreeing, 'Friends.'

They were both silent for a while, their hands tightly clasped.

At last he said awkwardly, 'Go on telling me about Sam.'

'He brought me up after my parents died, and he was always lovely to me. He had such plans for my future. You wouldn't think it to look at him now, but he was quite a slave-driver. He decided that I was going to college, and that was that.'

'You didn't get a say?'

'Oh, yes, I was allowed to choose what I wanted to study, but even then he had to take control. I said I'd like to do the history of art, and Sam said, "In that case you'll need to learn Italian". So I did.'

'You tamely did as you were told? *You?*'

'Well, I actually liked the idea a lot. I loved art, and I pick up languages easily, but I hadn't thought about college because we weren't an academic kind of family. Sam knew better. He simply took over, making me do my homework, and no nonsense. Then he declared war on junk food and insisted that I eat plenty of fruit.

'He also started doing a second job so that he could save money for me. He shouldn't have done that, it tired him out, but he was determined that I should have a nest-egg.'

She fell silent, looking into the distance.

'What happened?' Vittorio asked quietly.

'I took my exams, did well, won a place at a good college. And then—then Sam had a stroke. It wasn't very severe, and he recovered, but something had changed. He'd been getting absent-minded for some time, but only in little ways that we could joke about. Suddenly it was serious. He was forgetful about everything. I put off college, said I'd go next year, but I think I knew in my heart that it wouldn't happen.

'I got a job to support us, but I soon had to give that up. He kept leaving things on the stove. When he set fire to the house for the second time I left the job and stayed at home with him. We lived on his savings for a while.'

'The nest-egg for your college career?'

'That's right. When it ran out we had to rely on state benefits.'

'When did Ghastly Gavin enter the picture?'

Angel gave a choke of laughter. 'How do you know he was ghastly? You never met him.'

'I met him in the pages of that damned magazine, and he's ghastly all right.'

'Not to me, then. At nineteen all you see is looks, and his looks were gorgeous. I had sentimental fantasies of marriage, a happy home, with Sam making a third.

'Then I entered a television quiz show and won some money. I paid a few bills and bought Sam some new clothes. Gavin hit the roof. He wanted to splash out on a holiday. We had a row, he said it was time I had Sam "put away", so I kicked him right out of my life.'

'Good for you. But how does Joe Clannan come into this?'

'He had shares in the production company that made the programme. He was there during the recording, and he asked me out. I was still mad at Gavin and Joe seemed like a nice guy. We dated for a while, and when he proposed I accepted on the condition that Sam must live with us and have the best of care. Joe promised, and as long as he kept his word I was prepared to put on the performance he wanted.

'Even at the worst times I never quite gave up hope that one day I'd find my way back to my true path. You don't look at me and see an academic, do you? But that's how I've always felt inside, even when I was flaunting myself in the most vulgar fashion, plunging necklines, skirts slit up the thigh, perfectly timed wiggle. I practised that wiggle, you know, in front of the mirror, and, oh, boy, you should have seen me doing my stuff for the cameras!'

'I have,' Vittorio said, and could have bitten his tongue out straight afterwards.

'You mean some of those programmes have been shown over here? By satellite?'

'No, I got a video tape—when the sale had gone through...' he said awkwardly.

'What did you see?' she asked in a voice that gave him no clue as to how she was taking this.

*'Star On My Team.'*

'You mean—the one where I had to choose between Michelangelo and Maisie Mouse?' she asked unsteadily.

'That's the one.'

It was too much for her. Angel gave a choke, then exploded into laughter, leaning back against the slope of the lawn, gasping helplessly. Vittorio watched her, wryly remembering his violent reaction at the time.

'Come on, see the funny side,' she chided him when she could speak.

'I can. It's just that at the time I—well, let's just say it wasn't one of my better moments.'

'Don't tell me, let me guess. You got a little figure of an angel and stuck pins into it.' Seeing his embarrassment, she crowed, 'You did! Admit it!'

'I didn't, I swear—' Then he groaned. 'But only because I couldn't find an angel.'

She collapsed against him, chuckling helplessly, and he held her, finally able to laugh with her.

'You are the most forgiving woman,' he said unsteadily. 'And you shouldn't forgive me. I don't deserve it. If you only knew…'

'But I do know,' she said, her arms about his neck. 'You never bothered to hide it, even when you demanded the job. I'm not surprised you made a mess of it. It was a toss-up whether you loved this place more than you hated me.'

'I never hated you,' he said.

'Oh, yes you did.'

'No, that didn't happen,' Vittorio said, suddenly serious. 'It didn't happen because it couldn't.'

He took her face between his hands and looked at her tenderly.

'I could never hate you,' he said softly. 'Don't you know that?'

'I'm not sure that I do,' she whispered. 'Perhaps you should explain. I could take a lot of convincing.'

Even now something held him back. There was almost desperation in his eyes as he searched her face, knowing that whatever he did at this moment would be dangerous.

But Angel had reached the end of her tether. If he didn't kiss her now she knew she would do something stupid—and perhaps they would both be the better for it.

'If you can't explain,' she said, driven beyond endurance, 'then maybe I can.'

She made it all so simple, pulling his head down until his lips touched hers, moving her mouth softly against his, teasing him, but meaning it too, because the time for games was over.

'Angel,' he murmured. 'Angel…Angel…'

Now he wasn't merely invoking her name. In his arms, she felt like something both less and more than human—unearthly, magical, an angel, but with a little spice of the devil that was always going to be his undoing. Hadn't he known that from the start?

As he felt her using all her feminine power to make him hers, Vittorio made a last effort to stay aloof from the siren's song, to keep his soul his own as a man should. But he had no strength to fight her. Somewhere inside him, somewhere beyond words, deeper than conscious thought, he knew that victory would be defeat, and defeat would give him all he longed for.

Now she was stronger than him, every soft caress binding him like chains. She'd wanted him almost from the start, and only now did she understand how much.

But at the last moment he tensed and tried to draw back.

'Wait—this isn't right—I must tell you—'

'It's too late for that. There's nothing to tell.'

'I didn't mean this—we need to talk first— I'd better go home,' he said raggedly. 'Right now. Angel, please, don't make it hard for me to go.'

'But I don't want you to go,' she whispered, her

lips almost touching his face. 'And you don't want to—not really.'

'If I don't go now I won't be able to. Have you any idea just how badly I long to stay?'

'Why don't you show me?' she asked pointedly.

'Not now. Don't you understand that? After the things you've said about the men who pursue you in a herd—do you think I want to be one of that herd, tolerated but despised? You hate it, don't you—all the clowns who chase you with their eyes, and fantasise about going to bed with you?'

'Do you fantasise about going to bed with me?'

'No,' he said firmly. 'I do not.'

'Oh,' she breathed, deflated.

'What I dream about is making love to you. Since the first day I've wanted to…' a tremor went through him '…I've wanted things I knew I had no right to want. Why do you think I hated you? Because I *couldn't* hate you.'

Vittorio's voice was rising, and Angel raised her own to make herself heard. 'Will you stop talking?' she begged. 'Don't you know the time for that is way past?'

'Please listen—'

*'Oi!'*

They both froze, turning dismayed glances on the windows of Sam's room, from where the cry

had come. After a moment's silence it came
again, loud and indignant.

'Do you mind keeping it down? People are
trying to sleep here.'

'That's Sam,' Angel said, aghast. 'I forgot
we're right outside his room.'

'Does he understand Italian?'

'No—that is, I don't think so,' she said frantically. 'But I wouldn't put anything past him.'

There would never be a better chance to catch
Vittorio with his defences weakened. Taking him
by the hand, she drew him swiftly into the house
by a side door, and locked it after them.

'No more arguments,' she said. 'From now on,
we do it my way.'

Angel prided herself on being a realist, and she
knew that the problems were still there when she
awoke in the morning, but it was hard to think
about them after the night that had passed.

It had been as Vittorio promised, not a sex act
but lovemaking, infused with tenderness. Everything about him had taken her by surprise, starting
with the way he'd undressed her slowly, almost
with reverence, lingering over each revelation
before laying his lips against it.

When they had lain naked together he'd
touched her everywhere and she had been aston-

ished, both at him and at herself. His fingers had been skilled and gentle, lingering as he'd sensed her response, waiting for her, always giving her time, so that her desire mounted slowly.

She'd been overwhelmed as much by surprise as by passion. Eight years of marriage to an insensitive boor hadn't prepared her for a man who put her first all the time. There had been a moment of apprehension, when she'd feared that no dream could possibly live up to the weight of hope that she had loaded onto this one.

But he'd seemed to understand even that, meeting her eyes as he'd claimed her, smiling in reassurance, so that all fear had fallen away and she'd been free to yield herself to the mounting delight. She had known Vittorio as a man who knew how to hate. Now she'd discovered him as a man who knew how to love.

He was only the second naked man she had ever seen, Joe's flabby over-indulged form not having inspired her to explore further. She hadn't known that a man's body could be such a combination of strength and beauty, with dark hair lightly covering his chest down to his loins. Without his clothes he'd seemed more powerful, or perhaps that was merely her memory from the night, when his vigour had left her gasping and eager for more.

They'd seemed to fall asleep at the same moment, but she'd awoken later and had seen him, in the dim light, propped on his elbow, watching her.

'Go back to sleep,' he'd said. 'Everything's all right.'

And she'd fallen asleep at once, because everything truly was all right.

When she awoke again, she found him lying with his head against her breast.

'Are you awake?' she whispered.

'Yes. I've been lying here watching that crack of light in the shutters, wishing it wouldn't grow any brighter.'

'I know. I don't want the day to start either.' She looked at her bedside clock. 'But it's only just six.'

'I'm usually up by now.'

'Not today,' she murmured. 'I want a little longer, just like this.'

He gave a contented grunt that she took to indicate consent, and didn't speak for so long that she thought he'd fallen asleep again. But then he said, 'I didn't mean this to happen. I told myself I must not even think of it, but somehow—'

'I know. I tried to be strong too, but maybe I didn't really mean it.'

'I guess neither of us is strong.'

Angel laughed. 'Well, we're united about something anyway, and that's a miracle. At one time it choked you to speak to me.'

'I was angry at the world, and I took it out on you,' he confessed. 'And I was angry at myself because I brought so much of my misfortune on myself.'

'I thought it was Joe's fault.'

'In the second place, but in the first place it was my fault for being so easily taken in by a man I'd thought was a friend.'

'What happened?'

'His name is Leo Vari, and we'd known each other from childhood. He had a business that ran into trouble. He begged me to put some money into it, just to tide him over. He swore he wouldn't let me lose, no matter what happened. But when the business folded he vanished, and I found myself legally obliged to pay every penny he owed. There was only one way I could do it, and that was to sell up.'

'And then Joe cheated you again,' Angel said softly.

'If I could have got a fair price I might have had enough to make a new start. But then, I ask myself, what would I have done? Where would I have gone? I think I might still have returned here, because the estate has always been my life.

My father was a good man, and an affectionate father, but he had no gift for managing an estate. When I was twenty I took over, and he was relieved. He died five years later, but at least his last five years were happy because he wasn't worried.'

'But you had to worry,' she hazarded.

'I didn't mind. I enjoyed everything about it—turning it around financially, making the place bloom, working with my hands. There's no smell in the world like the earth in spring, when the rain has fallen and rebirth is happening just underground. And there's no feeling like watching something you planted grow and flower.'

He gave a short bark of self-mocking laughter.

'I thought my fiancée felt the same, but I guess that was foolish of me.'

'You're engaged?' she asked, horrified.

'Not any more, but I was once. It lasted two years. Then she got tired of waiting for the right moment, and I don't blame her. We were planning a big wedding, a romantic honeymoon cruise—'

'Just as soon as you could bear to be away for longer than five minutes,' Angel finished, amused.

'Yes, I guess that was it. She married a friend of mine and I'm godfather to their first child.'

'And there's been nobody else?'

'Oh, yes. Too many. I didn't want to get close

again, so I decided life would be simpler with only one love.'

'The estate.'

'Yes. I put all my eggs in one basket. I knew that was unwise, but when you love something that much you can't help yourself. My friend Bruno says I became obsessed and impossible to live with, and I guess he was right. I didn't care. I had the only thing that really mattered to me. I never asked about tomorrow. I suppose I thought that one day I'd meet a woman who felt about the estate as I did.'

'But it had to be on your terms?' she asked, amused.

'Those are the only terms I know how to accept. But what difference does it make now? What do I have to offer?'

'You want me to tell you?' she asked softly, with a smile that contained memories of the night.

Vittorio raised himself on one elbow and looked down into her face.

'I'm talking seriously.'

'So am I,' she said, taking his hand and laying it on her breast.

In the luxury of his lovemaking, she cared for nothing else. It was only later that she looked back and realised that his words had contained a warning.

# CHAPTER EIGHT

FOR A WHILE Angel had no time for anyone but Sam. She'd dreamt of the time when he would come here, she would show him his new home and they would be happy together, and now she would not accept that the dream could be spoiled.

She had been prepared for him to be sometimes confused, even not to know her, but this prolonged confusion and forgetfulness was a shock. Nonetheless, she argued it away. The long journey had been a strain, and he would soon return to some kind of normality. If only, she thought, it would happen soon.

It was strange to think that they had been apart for such a short time, because he seemed far more frail than she remembered, and she realised, with a sense of terror, that he was eighty-four.

He seemed happy enough. Each morning he greeted her pleasantly and waited while Frank or Roy introduced them all over again. He'd apparently decided that he was a guest in a pleasant country house and that she was his hostess. On this basis they had some cheerful talks. He asked her about her life and told her about his own early years, which he could recall with disconcerting clarity. It was only as he drew close to the present that the fog descended on his mind.

Sometimes he would chat about his beloved granddaughter, speaking of her with a love that made a lump come to Angel's throat.

'I haven't seen her for a while,' he said once, sounding puzzled and a little hurt. 'She used to visit me a lot but now—do you think she might be angry with me?'

'Of course not,' Angel said, trying to speak brightly. 'I'm sure she loves you very much.'

'Then why doesn't she call me any more?' he asked sadly.

'She's probably on her way here to see you,' Angel said desperately.

'That's what I keep thinking, but she never comes.'

She could hardly bear it when Sam said that. Later, when he was having his afternoon nap, Angel slipped out of the house and ran to the lemon terraces, where she knew Vittorio would be. It was a place she usually avoided after her fall, but today nothing mattered except to talk to him, and she climbed hurriedly down.

Taking one look at her face, Vittorio said not a word, but held her in his arms until she stopped shaking.

'Was it very bad today?' he asked.

'He was telling me about his granddaughter, how much he loves her and—and how hurt he is that she doesn't come to see him. And all the time he's sitting looking at me—and he doesn't know me.'

'But he will,' Vittorio said. 'You told me yourself that this happens sometimes, but then his memory comes back. You have to hang on for those moments.'

'I know, I know. It's just—'

'Why don't you take a day off? We'll drive, just have a few hours together.'

'I couldn't leave him alone.'

'He's not alone. He's got the lads, and you know he's fine with them.'

'He's better with them than he is with me,' Angel sighed. 'But still…'

What made her decide in the end was that Roy said much the same thing.

'All the time you're with him you're tense,' he told her. 'He can sense it, and it makes him tense too. You should take a few hours off, go and do some shopping.'

'I'll think about it.'

When Sam greeted her next morning, still with no sign of recognition, she took a deep breath and announced that she was going out for a while. She almost ran to where Vittorio had told her he would be in the garden.

As soon as he saw her coming he understood. By the time she reached the place where he'd parked his shabby car, he was holding the door open for her as elegantly as a chauffeur with a limousine.

'What is the *padrona*'s pleasure?' he enquired, getting behind the wheel.

'You can stop that *padrona* nonsense, and just take me to a coffee shop.'

'As the *padrona* wishes.'

'I'm warning you.'

He grinned and started up.

Amalfi stood at the foot of the cliffs, a little town that went back more than a thousand years. Once it had been an important trading centre, economically way ahead of the rest of Italy, and an independent republic until the twelfth century. Now, although its great trading days were past, it still flourished, attracting visitors who fell in love with the beauty of its picturesque streets and the pleasures to be found on its beach.

Vittorio found a little coffee shop and plied Angel with ice-cream sundaes, as though she were a child on a treat. While she was eating, he said, 'Wait here,' and went outside, returning a moment later with a glossy magazine.

'The shop next door specialises in English publications for the tourists,' he said, 'and I thought it was worth a try. Your journalist friend didn't waste any time.'

The magazine was the new edition of *Glam-Chick*, the cover sporting one of the pictures Mack had shown her of Joe with his bride on his arm. There were two tag lines, one announcing, *Joe Clannan weds another beauty* and the other saying, *How I feel about Joe's wedding: Angel reveals all*.

'Well, that's a lie,' she said indignantly. 'I never said a thing about the wedding except the most boring platitudes.'

Vittorio was reading over her shoulder. 'You didn't utter boring platitudes about Gavin,' he observed.

'But I did.'

He began to read. '"Angel is particularly incensed about the recent feature in which the lover she dumped—"'

'Lover, my left foot!' she seethed.

'"The lover she dumped…"' Vittorio continued, silencing her. '..."spoke for the first time of his heartbreak at losing her to wealthy Joe Clannan. According to Angel, Gavin is fantasising. In fact she can hardly remember him. 'He was history before I met Joe,' she said sweetly. 'Not that he was ever anything much. Everything about Gavin was limited, starting with his conversation.' Modesty prevented her *enlarging* on this subject, but clearly Gavin wasn't impressive *in any way*."'

Vittorio leaned back, regarding her with humorous appreciation. 'You sure got your revenge.'

'But I didn't,' she exploded. 'I just said his conversation was limited, and they've dressed it up with all those suggestive hints.'

'Never mind. Serves him right after what he said about you.'

'Yes, I don't feel very guilty about it either. It was clever of them to get both features in the one issue, wasn't it? They must have moved fast.'

She studied her 'tell-all' piece, realising that the glossy creature in the pictures was a stranger. That was fine by her. Then she turned her attention to the wedding pictures, which she regarded with a wry smile.

'You're not upset?' Vittorio asked, watching her.

'Only by having my name associated with all

that purple prose. Never mind. I got the cheque this morning. It'll keep the wolves from the door.'

'Perhaps you shouldn't have given him back the jewellery,' Vittorio observed mildly. 'You were too generous there.'

Angel regarded him with an amusement that had a touch of the hysterical.

'Don't you understand Joe better than that yet? I didn't give him back anything. He took it all out of the bank and hid it before he ever mentioned divorce.'

'Of course. I should have thought of that.'

'Those jewels belong to Mrs Joe Clannan, *whoever she happens to be at the time*. In effect, on loan. When I no longer suited his require-ments, he called the loan in. Now it's Merry's turn.' She looked at the picture of the smirking, diamond-laden girl. 'Poor thing.'

'You can feel sorry for her?'

'She thinks she's got it all, but she doesn't know what's going to hit her.'

They wandered the streets aimlessly, not heading for any particular place but happy in each other's company. Angel had been to Amalfi several times, but always alone. Seeing it with Vittorio was different. The great tenth-century cathedral was where his parents had married, the beach was where he had played as a child.

'You could do with a day in the sun,' he said as they strolled along the waterfront. 'We'll take a boat and sail to a little cove I know where we can picnic and bathe and…' he shrugged expressively '…enjoy ourselves any way we like.'

His smile brought back memories of their night together. It had been more than a week ago, and with everything in her she longed to make love with him again. But now things had changed.

'I can't,' she said sadly. 'I have to be there for Sam.'

'But he doesn't know you.'

'His head might suddenly clear at any moment. I took today off, but it'll be ages before I can do it again.' She met his eyes. 'Don't think I don't want to, because I do, but…' She sighed. 'When I told you everything was for Sam, I really meant it.'

He gave her a rueful grin. 'I know you did. I guess I'm just being selfish. I don't like it when it's me that's called on to make a sacrifice.'

'You're not the only one who feels deprived,' she murmured. Then a thought struck her. 'Didn't you tell me that you live in Amalfi? If your place is near here—'

'It isn't,' he said quickly. 'It's too far—and it isn't tidy.'

'As though I'd care—'

'It's getting late. I'll take you home,' he said, in a voice that brooked no refusal.

At the villa Vittorio bid Angel a civil good-night, but wouldn't stay for supper. He had suddenly become tense in a way she didn't understand.

She discovered the answer later, when she was talking to Berta in the kitchen as Berta put the final touches to the evening meal.

'Do you know where Vittorio lives now?' Angel asked. 'I thought it was in Amalfi, but maybe I misheard.'

'No, it's Amalfi,' Berta said. 'He's got a couple of rooms in…' She named a street and shuddered. 'Horrible.'

'You've been there?'

'I helped him move his things, but most of them he had to leave behind, the place is so small. To think that he was once master here, and now he tries to survive in that mean little place. *Ai, ai, ai!*'

So that was it. Vittorio was too proud to let her see the depths to which he had fallen. She should have realised.

'Don't tell him I asked,' Angel said.

'Of course not, *signora*.' Berta hadn't intended

to say a word. She was a wise woman who understood far more than she said.

Sam was tetchy over his meal, and had an early night. When he was safely asleep, Roy and Frank tackled her.

'He's bored,' Frank explained. 'In England he used to watch television a lot, but now he's missing all his favourite programmes, especially the soaps.'

'He missed the episode of *Celebration Road* where we find out if old Mrs Baxter really did put arsenic on her husband's breakfast cereal,' Roy said. 'And he's inconsolable.'

'So are we,' Frank added significantly.

Light dawned.

'And you are also missing your favourite TV shows?' Angel said.

They looked at each other and nodded.

'She's bright,' they agreed.

'Oh, heck, I should have thought of this,' she said. 'Since I can watch Italian programmes, it never occurred to me.'

'Seriously,' Roy said, 'he's used to spending hours in front of the set. Now that he can't understand a word, he's miserable.'

'I'll sort it tomorrow,' she promised.

Next day she made a call to a firm that specialised in satellite installations, and the day after that a team arrived to set up a system that could pick up English television. Everyone was pleased, especially Sam, who was able to resume his comforting routine, and who finally discovered that old Mrs Baxter had played no part in her husband's untimely end. This made him very happy. He had always liked that poor lady.

Now Angel could spend time with Vittorio with a clear conscience. As promised, he hired a boat and took her sailing. Watching her leaning back, her face upturned to the sun, he smiled but said nothing, concentrating on steering the boat. After a while he headed for the shore, where there was a small cove with a stretch of perfect sand.

'Let's stop here,' he said. 'Swim first, picnic afterwards.'

They pulled the boat far up the sand and stripped off their clothes. Beneath her cotton top and jeans she wore a black bikini, ready for bathing. It had been designed to be elegant and glamorous, and for the first time she was glad of the way it showed her off. The others had shamed her, but Vittorio's eyes made her proud.

When Vittorio had discarded his own clothes, they ran, hand in hand, into the sea.

'Oh, wonderful!' she crowed as the cool water enveloped her. 'Wonderful, wonderful!'

'Mind the current,' he called. 'It's strong here.'

'I'm all right,' she said, swimming away from him into deeper water.

He came after her at once, catching her and putting his hands on her waist.

'You're not all right,' he said firmly. 'You have to be careful here.'

'*You* find it safe enough,' she said, wriggling against his grip, less because she wanted to be free than because she enjoyed moving against him. It was even more pleasurable when his hands tightened.

'I'm safe because I know this place, and I'm careful. You know nothing and you're never careful.' With a touch of humour he added, 'It's your way to plunge recklessly into unknown situations. I've told you about that before.'

'Yes, you did. I seem to remember...' she teased '...something to do with lemons, wasn't it?' She slipped her arms about his neck, pressing him close and moving more intimately.

'Don't do that in deep water,' he protested. 'Do you want us both to drown?'

'We won't drown,' she said against his mouth. 'You'll keep us safe.'

'You have too much faith in me,' he said, speaking with difficulty.

'Well, who wants to be safe anyway?' she

asked recklessly. 'Let the current carry us out to sea, then, wherever it wants.'

He drew a long breath. 'Wherever it wants,' he repeated longingly.

'Anywhere,' she said. 'We won't plan anything, because if you don't make plans you don't have to worry about them going wrong. Do you know how much I hate plans, and calculations, and working out what to say so that someone will respond with the right words?'

'Hush,' he said, brushing her lips with his own. 'That's all behind you.'

'Is it?' she asked, almost pleading. 'And them? All of them? Are they behind me?'

He didn't have to ask who 'they' were: all the men who'd thronged around her, devouring her with their eyes and their thoughts, thinking they owned her or, at any rate the little bit of her that was all they cared about.

'They're in the past,' he assured her. 'For ever.'

'They can't get me again, can they?'

'No, because I won't let them.'

She was suddenly full of fear. 'Don't let them find me, ever again.'

'I never will. Never. Never.'

He held her close, not kissing her but keeping her safe, while he trod water for both of them, until the force of the current made him say unsteadily, 'Let's go back while we still can. Being swept away together sounds fine, but I'm hungry.'

'And we have that picnic basket Berta packed for us.'

'I didn't mean for food.'

Angel laughed, and they made their way back. As they ran up the beach Vittorio seized the towel and followed her into the cave, where they dried each other off and removed their clothes at the same time.

They made love urgently, as though they could make up for the days apart, and when it was over they were immediately ready again, but this time it was slower, gentler, with more time to explore and enjoy. The sand was soft against her back, and she could taste the sea on her own lips, and his.

Now it felt like the taste of freedom, something she hadn't known for years—freedom to be herself, to choose her own lover, to respond to him with total liberty of heart. The physical pleasure he brought her was sweet, but almost as intense was the fact that she had chosen him. Every whisper, every movement, was like a gift that he gave her from his soul.

'Again,' she pleaded. 'Again.'

He smiled. 'Do I please you?'

Her answering smile told him all he needed to know. It was leisurely, contented, luxurious, and it brought his desire flooding back, so that he loved her now as though they had been apart for weeks.

'I'm sorry,' he said at last, in a shaking voice. 'I didn't mean to lose control.'

'I don't know what you're apologising for,' she murmured, laughing up at him.

'Siren,' he said. 'Witch—temptress—angel…'

He sat up, but when Angel tried to rise also Vittorio placed a hand on her breast and gently pushed her back.

'No,' he said. 'Stay there and let me look at you.'

She lay back, stretching her arms above her head, gladly putting her beauty on show for him, and rejoicing at his adoring gaze. It was as though his eyes were touching her, giving soft caresses that thrilled her body as much as his fingertips had done.

She was perfect. She had always been perfect, but this was different. Now it was only for him, and that knowledge seemed to wash away the memories of the other times, when she had been put on display to satisfy Joe Clannan's vanity.

Vittorio had promised to banish the past for her, and at that moment she truly believed that he could do it.

There was nothing to warn her of the pit that was about to open at her feet.

They put their swimsuits back on before going out into the sun, spread a blanket on the sand, and took out the basket full of wine, rolls and cakes. On this they dined like princes, content simply to be there with each other, asking no more.

When they had finished eating, Angel took a long, blissful breath and rolled over on her back, her head turned up to the sky, her eyes closed.

'You look like a little kid discovering all this for the first time,' Vittorio said, grinning. 'Have you ever been sailing before?'

'Oh, yes,' she said, without opening her eyes. 'Joe thought the summer was wasted if we didn't spend it on some millionaire's yacht.' She chuckled. 'Heavens, it was boring! I used to take ten swimsuits and none of them ever got wet. They were all for lounging by the pool "on show".'

When Vittorio didn't answer, Angel opened her eyes to find him looking at her with a dark expression.

'Like the one you're wearing now?' he asked quietly.

'This was one of them, yes. I haven't bought any new clothes recently. I'm making the old ones last. In the old days I just threw them away.'

'Be quiet,' he said softly. 'Never talk of those days to me. Do you think I want to hear how you paraded yourself in front of other men?'

Suddenly there was a hard, ugly note in his voice and it shocked her into sitting up, staring at him in dismay and disbelief.

'I did not parade myself,' she said firmly. 'Joe paraded his trophy wife and I acted a part. I had no choice. That wasn't really me—'

'It was *your* body that they were looking at. How do you think that makes me feel?'

'Probably the same way it made me feel,' she said, trying to keep her temper. 'I hated it.'

'But you did it.'

Icy fingers were going up and down her spine, and suddenly the air was full of threat.

'You know why I did it,' she said. 'Vittorio, how dare you start getting possessive about something that happened before we met? In those days I didn't know you existed. I didn't owe you anything, and I don't owe you explanations now.'

His eyes were dark, unfathomable, but there was no doubting the cold bitterness in his voice.

'I shouldn't be possessive? What do you think I am? An Englishman, saying, "Yes, dear—no, dear—just as you please, dear"? If you belong to me, you belong *to me*. Do you understand?'

'I understand that you're starting to act like Joe,' Angel said, her temper flaring. 'And I don't like it. I had eight years of being a piece of property, dancing to the tune of a man who

thought he could own and control me, and it's not
going to happen again. I don't belong to you, or
any man, and I never will. That wasn't me back
then. I was a different person.'

'You pretend it was—'

'It's the truth—'

'In your mind, maybe, but there's one part of
you for which it can't be true.'

His eyes travelled slowly over her body that the
minute bikini left almost naked, his meaning unmistakable.

'Don't look at me like that,' she choked.

'I have loved looking at you. You body is more
beautiful than I could have believed possible, and
I guess the others thought so too, because it's the
same b—'

'Don't,' she said swiftly, putting her hand over
his mouth. 'Don't say that.'

'Will not saying it make a difference?'

Angel stared at him, sickened by this sudden
development that had happened without warning.
They had made love in peace and joy, and then
she had lain, innocently naked, before his adoring
gaze. The aftermath should have been beautiful.
Yet a moment had transformed him into an ugly,
judgemental stranger.

'You're right,' she said in a stony voice. 'It's
*thinking* it that makes a difference, and I'll never

forgive you for that. My God, it's only an hour or so ago that you said those men were in the past, that they couldn't get me again because you'd protect me. But they *will* get me again, because they'll come through you, and every man like you. They *are* you.'

Her voice cracked with anguish as the full horror of the truth burst on her. 'Do you see what you've done? You've shown me that there's no way out for me. I am what Joe Clannan made me. I thought I could escape, but I never can as long as men see me through that distorting prism. And you're a man like any other. I thought you were different, but you're not. The truth is that no man is ever different. It's lucky we found out now, isn't it?'

Vittorio could neither answer nor look at her. His face was dark, heavy with the thoughts he couldn't bear to utter. She picked up her clothes and went into the little cave. Now she only wanted to hide her body from him. He made her feel ugly and ashamed.

When she came out he was dressed and putting things into the boat. In silence they pushed it into the sea, and got aboard.

Not a word was spoken as they sailed back to Amalfi. At any other time she would have rejoiced in the journey, with the sun turning the sea to fire. It was a scene to make lovers rejoice, but they were no longer lovers. A black shadow had fallen between them, and Angel had a terrible fear that it would stretch over the rest of her life.

# CHAPTER NINE

STILL IN SILENCE they got into Vittorio's car and finished the journey back to the estate. Bitterness seethed in Angel. She wanted to rend him and break his heart as he had broken hers.

After this, she would be as calculating as he clearly thought that she was. She would dismiss him from her employment, but not at once. First she must learn everything he could teach her. She would pick his brains clean. Then, when she was strong enough to manage without him, she would throw him out.

He thought she'd been marked by her previous life. Fine! He would discover that she really had been marked, but not in the way that he thought. Revenge would be sweet, she promised herself, and the thought sustained her the rest of the way.

When the house came into sight she said quietly, 'I'll get out here.'

'It's getting dark. Let me take you a little closer.'

'Stop the car, *right now*.'

He did so, and watched as she got out and walked away. She didn't look back until she was nearly at the house, and then his tail lights were already vanishing into the distance.

In her room she stripped off and showered, scrubbing herself repeatedly, as though she could scrub off the day and everything that had happened. But there was no way to wash away the feel of Vittorio holding her, or the look in his eyes when he'd turned against her. She would remember that look all her life, and hate him for it until the last moment.

She pulled on a towel robe and returned to the bedroom, switching off the light so that she could go and stand at the window. The moon had risen high, casting a silver sheen on the ocean beneath, giving it a look of unearthly peace.

It was no different from any other night, Angel thought wretchedly. That chill, indifferent tranquillity would endure no matter whose heart broke. And perhaps it was better to let her heart break now than put off facing the truth until later. What had happened today had always been bound to happen.

A movement from below made her look down, wondering if Toni had been locked out. But he was there beside her, paws on the window sill.

Who, then, was below?

When she looked out again the moon had gone behind a cloud, filling the garden with darkness, until the cloud passed and she saw who was standing there. Vittorio was gazing up at her and, even in this light, she thought she'd never seen so much misery in a human face—greater, even, than her own.

'I thought you'd gone home,' she called down softly.

He simply shook his head.

'Go to the kitchen door,' she said.

He was there by the time she reached it and pulled back the bolts. But when she pulled open the door and stood back for him to pass he made no move. She couldn't see his face, but the tension was there in every line of him.

'Come in,' she said, turning to lead the way, and leaving him to lock the door.

Outside the bedroom door he stood back, again refusing to enter until she summoned him, and even then asking, 'Are you sure that I may?'

'Come in,' she said.

He came across the threshold as though fearful, and when she'd closed the door he made no move to touch her.

'How long had you been out there?'

'I got halfway home before I turned around. I

had to come back and ask—*beg* your forgiveness. I don't deserve it. I don't know what I was thinking of…'

The moment he said 'beg your forgiveness' it was all over. Angel placed her fingers over his lips, feeling all pain and anger dissolve, and drew him further inside the room, so that she could sit down on the bed. But instead of sitting beside her he dropped to his knees.

'Forgive me,' he said hoarsely. 'I never meant to speak to you so. I know you are innocent, but inside me I am insane with jealousy. I try not to be. I know that none of it was your fault, but reason has no place in the way I feel about you. Nothing and nobody in the world has ever mattered to me as you do. It frightens me how much you matter. I don't know what to do.'

'Must you do anything?' Angel whispered. 'Is it so terrible for me to matter?'

'In a way it is,' Vittorio said sombrely. 'Love isn't simple for me. Today—with you in my arms—such joy, such beauty…greater than I have ever known. You seemed to have taken possession of me, as though my soul were no longer my own.'

A tremor went through him, and she guessed that this was what he feared so much that it tinged love with dread.

And perhaps he was right, Angel thought sadly. She had felt the same, as though he had taken possession of her, and it had made the pain of his hostility all the greater. Wouldn't it be better to do as he did, and retreat to safety?

But the next moment she knew better. There was no safety for either of them.

'I turned on you to protect myself.' He sighed, resting his head against her. 'It's the only way I knew to escape you.'

'If you want to escape me that much, perhaps you should.'

He looked into her face. 'You would send me away?'

'I wouldn't keep you against your will. Vittorio, one part of you still hates me—'

'*No!*' he said violently.

'Yes. It's the truth. If I can admit it, why can't you?'

He gave a wintry smile. 'Because you have more courage than me. Do you think I don't know that? I could never truly hate you, not now. But I want so many different things at once—to flee from you, to lose myself in you. Sometimes I think it can never be right for us. There's too much holding us apart. But then I look at you and I know that nothing must come between us.'

'I guess we both have our demons,' she said. 'And they're always lying in wait. But just now, let's forget them.'

'Say that you forgive me,' Vittorio whispered.

'There is nothing to forgive.' Angel stroked his face. 'We have to be generous with each other. There's no other way for us.'

Angel took his face between her hands and kissed him tenderly. 'We can make it right now,' she murmured.

But when she tried to put her arms around him he drew back and rose to his feet.

'Not now,' he said. 'It's too soon—I don't trust myself...'

'But if I trust you?'

'You mustn't,' he said with sudden frantic urgency. 'If I were strong enough I'd go far away and leave you in peace—but I can't, except for just a little while.'

'Stay,' she murmured against his mouth.

'I can't—I mustn't—'

'Stay.'

She could feel his indecision, the terrible fight he was waging inside his divided self, and for a moment she was sure she'd won. But at the last minute he pulled away.

'Forgive me,' he said hoarsely.

And fled.

* * *

Angel had a poor night, and went down next morning feeling weary and disgruntled. But a pleasant surprise awaited her.

Through the window she saw Sam walking in the garden on Roy's arm. She went out, bracing herself for the painful moment when he wouldn't know her, but to her joy his face lit up and he waved.

'Angela, darling!' he cried, opening his arms. 'It's lovely to see you again. Where have you been all this time?'

'I've been around,' she said cautiously. At all costs she didn't want to say anything that would trouble him.

'You should have come to see me. I've missed you so much.'

'Never mind, we're together now. That's all that matters.'

'But where are we, my dear? I don't seem to know this place.'

'Come and have breakfast, and we'll talk.'

To her delight, Sam continued to be cheerful and clear-headed over breakfast. Angel told him about the divorce and he nodded in approval.

'I wondered why I hadn't seen Joe around recently. I never did like him, you know.'

'If you want the truth, neither did I,' she confided, and they laughed like conspirators.

He was Sam again. Her Sam. The twinkle was

back in his eye and the warmth in his gaze as it rested on her.

'Later I'll show you the estate,' she said. 'You're going to love Italy.'

'This is Italy?' He beamed. 'But that's wonderful. We always planned for you to come here to study art, remember?'

'Yes, I do. And you remember? You really do?'

'Of course I remember, you silly girl. As though I could forget a thing like that!'

Afterwards they went walking through the garden and he admired the flowers. Angel was overflowing with happiness, praying for this time to last.

Toni, who'd taken an instant liking to Sam, was bounding joyfully around him, although some instinct seemed to warn him against colliding with the frail old man. Then a distant bark alerted Toni to Luca, and the next moment the two dogs were racing for each other.

'Who's that?' Sam asked, pointing to the man working at the end of a row of rose bushes.

'That's Vittorio.'

She was slightly nervous as he came towards them, wondering if Sam would recall their first meeting and connect him with the distress of the journey home. But Sam was smiling.

'We've met before, haven't we?' he said.

'Well, yes…' Vittorio began cautiously, looking at Angel for guidance. 'I was—'

'No, don't tell me, let me guess. I'm a bit forgetful sometimes, but I like to remember for myself, if I can. I know, you drove me home. That must be some time ago now.'

'Just a couple of weeks,' Vittorio said.

'Jolly good. Jolly good. So you're Vittorio?'

'I work for the *signora*,' he said gravely.

'Well, I'm Sam. Oh, but of course, we've met, haven't we? Have you brought all these roses on? Done a great job. I used to grow roses. You must come and talk to me about them.'

'Come now,' Angel said.

It was the start of an odd friendship. Sam and Vittorio took to each other, and over the next few days they had long conversations, apparently in total understanding. It was good to see her grandfather happy, but now Angel never seemed to have more than a moment alone with Vittorio. All the time he was either occupied with Sam or hard at work.

'It will be harvest soon,' he said. 'And you want everything to be at its best.'

'I might think you were still avoiding me,' she suggested.

He gave her a brief kiss.

'No, I want us to be together, but I won't neglect my duty, even for you.'

'What about your duty *to* me?'

He grinned. 'I thought Sam came first?'

'He does, it's just—I miss you.'

It was a disconcerting part of Sam's problem that he wasn't equally confused about everything. He could still remember every funny story he'd ever heard, especially the rude ones, as Vittorio remarked with relish. And his ability to play chess was unimpaired. He'd trounced Roy and Frank so often that there was no more pleasure in it, and when he discovered that Vittorio was an expert player he fell on him with delight.

'Thank you for being so kind to him,' Angel said once. 'I love hearing him laugh with you.'

'I'm not being kind. I enjoy his company. He's fantastic. And he can beat me at chess.'

'I wondered if you were letting him win.'

'Well, I'm not,' he said in a chagrined voice. 'And stop laughing.'

'I can't help it. It's so wonderful to see him happy.'

'He really is the only person in the world whom you care for, isn't he?'

She touched his face. 'You know better than that.'

With such moments they got by, sometimes

stealing some time alone together, but more often having to be satisfied with being in the same room in the company of others. Sam's friendship had made Vittorio part of the family, and it was a rare evening when he didn't join them to watch television, play chess and study Angel silently.

Rescue came in the form of a weekend of *Celebration Road*, which Sam was determined not to miss.

'Episodes from the archives,' he explained. 'Some of them haven't been seen for years, so you won't disturb me, will you, darling?'

'I promise,' Angel said fervently. 'Would you—would you mind if I was away overnight?'

'Anything you like, darling. Oh, look, it's starting!'

Leaving him blissfully content, she was able to escape with Vittorio to wander the streets of Amalfi, doing little, saying less, needing nothing but each other. They stopped off in a newsagent, and while he bought a paper she looked around the shop and noticed a poster, advertising a lottery with a big roll-over prize that week.

'Hey, I want to enter that,' she said. 'One ticket, please.'

'Me too,' Vittorio called. 'Will you get me one?'

'What about the numbers?'

'You pick them for me.'

She bought two tickets, giving two sets of six numbers, and joined him on the way out of the shop.

'Here's your…' she began to say, but he interrupted her, pointing to where a horse and carriage waited by the kerb, the driver looking around hopefully.

'That's the best way to travel,' Vittorio said.

'Lovely!'

It was a charming vehicle, painted yellow with blue and white cushions, and a large sunshade. He handed her aboard, calling, 'Anywhere!' to the driver, who hopped up behind the horse, which set off.

'I've seen these when I've been here before,' Angel said in delight, as the horse trotted through tiny, winding streets. 'I've always wanted to take one. Oh, I forgot, your ticket.'

He gave her the price of one ticket and she said, 'Which one do you want?'

He shrugged. 'You choose.'

Holding them up in one hand she began to intone, 'Eeeny, meeny—*hey*!'

The yell was jerked from her as the carriage jolted hard, throwing her against him, and depositing the tickets onto the floor.

'We went over a stone,' Vittorio laughed, helping her up. 'Are you all right?'

'Sure, fine. It was just a bit unexpected. Vittorio?'

Suddenly she had lost his attention. He was staring over her shoulder, twisting his head further as the carriage moved on.

'What's the matter?' she asked.

'It's him,' he said. 'It's *him*!'

'Who?'

'Leo. My so-called friend who cheated me out of everything I had. I saw him…'

'Are you sure? Where?'

'There—no—in that street—driver, go that way, fast.'

The driver swore and began to back up.

'Hurry!' Vittorio shouted.

'I have to turn the horse, *signore*,' the driver shouted back indignantly.

Vittorio swore under his breath. 'I can't wait. He mustn't get away from me.' He flashed a glance at Angel. 'Forgive me!'

Then he was gone, vaulting out of the carriage and tearing back down the road until he vanished down a side street.

'Follow him,' Angel called frantically to the driver. 'Keep him in sight.'

At last the horse managed to turn, gather speed,

and head for the street, arriving just in time for her to see Vittorio at the far end. In another moment he'd turned the corner and vanished.

'Can't you go any faster?' she urged.

'She is not a racehorse, *signora*.'

After what seemed like an age they reached the end of the street and found themselves facing the little harbour. There was no sign of Vittorio and nothing to show in which direction he'd gone.

'Where now?' the driver asked, drawing to a halt.

'I don't know. He's vanished. I don't know where he could be now.'

'Some people will do anything to avoid paying,' the man said cynically.

'That's not—'

'I suppose he took your purse with him. It's the oldest trick in the book.'

'How dare you say that?' she flashed, furious at his cynical judgement. 'You know nothing about him.'

'I know that he ran away without paying.'

'Here's your money.'

Angel pulled out some notes and pushed them into his hand before jumping out of the carriage. At the last moment she reached back for the lottery tickets which were still lying, unnoticed, on the floor.

But when she was alone there was a sense of anti-climax. What was she supposed to do now? Vittorio could have gone in either direction, and even if she turned the right way there were a hundred streets to choose from. She could be wandering for hours.

But at least walking would help calm her temper, which had risen to boiling point. The driver's slander of Vittorio had caused an explosion inside her, astonishing in its force. What amazed her most was that she discovered how much of it was protectiveness.

He was the last man she would have thought of as needing protection: a hard man, unyielding, unforgiving, confident in his own knowledge and strength, his own power to dominate. That was Vittorio.

But then the need to stand between him and the world's harsh judgement had come surging out of nowhere, shaking her, making her almost ready to kill to defend him. And suddenly she'd understood how vulnerable he was, more than he knew.

She had rejoiced in the passion that united them. Now she discovered that the longing to protect could be as powerful as desire, and far sweeter.

For the first time she dared to use the word love, and wonder at it. Her life had involved so much falseness, so many games of pretended love, that now she wondered if she could recognise the real thing. She only knew that she could not bear Vittorio to be hurt.

It was for that reason that she stayed there, going from street to street, while the daylight faded and the lamps came on, and all the while her heart was with him, wandering somewhere, tortured by a mixture of hope and despair.

At last she gave up and made her way back to the car. And there he was, sitting on a low wall, his hands clasped between his knees, his head sunk. Angel dropped beside him, slipping an arm around his shoulders.

'You didn't catch him?'

He shook his head. His body was trembling and she could feel his exhaustion.

'Are you sure it was him?' she asked gently.

Vittorio shook his head.

'No, I can't even be sure of that. I see him everywhere, but I never find him. It's useless, hopeless.'

'That's not true. Nothing's ever completely hopeless,' she said, knowing how empty the words really were.

He took her hand.

'I ran off and left you without warning, and you couldn't even get into the car because I had the key. Why aren't you angry with me?'

'I guess I just can't manage that. Besides, I could have called a taxi.'

'You should have.'

'No, I couldn't go off and leave you alone while you were in trouble.'

He squeezed her hand. 'You should have done,' he said. 'Let the madman wander on his own, until he wises up enough to know that he's beyond help.'

'Don't talk like that.'

'How else should I talk?'

'You're forgetting the lottery. You might win.'

He managed a faint grin. 'Yes, I suppose I might win, but somehow I don't think I'll count on it.' He gave her a weary smile that broke her heart. 'Are you sure you wouldn't like to get angry at me?'

'Not now. I haven't the energy. Nor have you, from the look of you. When did you last eat?'

He shrugged.

'There's a little place over there. Come on.'

Vittorio was almost too tired to move, but Angel took charge, drawing him firmly to his feet and towards the little trattoria. They managed spaghetti, wine and coffee. They didn't speak. She would gladly have talked but she could tell that he was silent not only because he was tired, but because he was exhausted to the point of emptiness. It was as if he had been hollowed out inside, leaving only a barely functioning shell. So she left him in peace.

'I'll drive you home,' Vittorio said at last.

'You're not driving anywhere tonight,' Angel said. 'Tell me where you live. I'm going to take you there. You need to collapse, and the sooner the better.'

'No,' he said at once. 'Not there.'

'Then I'll take you back to the estate.'

'And sleep in your room? The *padrona* is too kind.'

'Then you can have a room of your own. You should have one anyway, so that you don't have to come all the way back here when you've been working late, which you often do, and…'

The words died at the look he gave her.

'You are offering me a room in that house? A temporary room, of course, and only when the work justifies it.'

'Don't,' she whispered. 'Please don't.'

His shoulders sagged. 'I'm sorry. It's unforgivable of me to take it out on you, especially when you're being so kind. I know that, but I do it anyway, and I probably can't stop. I warned you.'

'Warning duly noted,' she said tenderly. 'Now, you're tired, and I'm taking you home.'

He gave a faint, wry smile. 'Which home is that?'

'The one here in Amalfi, because it's nearest and you need to get to bed. No more argument. It's settled.'

'Giving me orders?'

'Yes.'

'And if I refuse to give you the address?'

For an answer, Angel simply laid her hand over his, looking at him tenderly.

'All right,' he said.

There was no pleasure in her small victory. The cost to him was too high.

Following his directions, she found her way to a tiny, narrow street, and even in the semi-darkness she could see enough to dismay her. Berta had warned her of the worst, and the worst was true. Inside she found the meanest rooms in the meanest house in the meanest street.

Somehow the atmosphere was even more depressing with the light on. There was one main room, which doubled as bedroom and living room, with a tiny alcove that did duty as a kitchen, and a bathroom that looked like a converted cupboard.

The man who had once owned the Villa Tazzini now lived here. No wonder he'd been ashamed for her to see it. She wondered if he would have more bitter words, but he only looked at her without speaking.

'You should go,' he said. 'I'll call a taxi.'

She shook her head. 'I'm not leaving you alone tonight.'

He managed a half-smile, full of wry defeat. 'I'm good for nothing now.'

'I didn't mean that. I want us to talk.' She took him by the shoulders. 'We never have talked. We've fought and quarrelled and loved, but never simply talked as friends.'

'Friends?'

'We said once we were friends. We have to be that, too. Don't you see?'

A gentle push made him sit down on the narrow bed. He didn't speak at first, and she had to prompt him.

'You told me about Leo, the friend who cheated you, but you didn't say much about him. It doesn't sound like you to be taken in, even by a friend.'

'I trusted him totally. I'd known him all my life. Years ago we got into mischief together, courted the same girls and compared notes later.'

'Shocking,' Angel said fondly.

'True. I was a rather disreputable character in those days.'

'You and every young man who's ever lived.

I'd have liked to know you in your disreputable days.'

'You wouldn't. I was a rogue,' he replied.

'But I thought you devoted your whole life to running the estate. You made yourself sound like a positive puritan.'

'If I did, I lied. I worked hard, but I had my fun. My father had to bail me out a few times.'

'For what?'

'The usual.'

'Drunk and disorderly?'

'Things like that, yes. Innocent fun. Leo was always there with me, and that's when the firmest bonds were formed. With anyone else I'd have been on my guard, but when he guaranteed my safety I believed him. And when he turned out to be wrong, even then I'd have forgiven him if he hadn't vanished and left me to face everything alone. I was easy prey for the creditors because I knew nothing. He'd taken the books with him. All that was left was a mess.'

Vittorio threw himself back on the bed, staring at the ceiling as though he could see his life being played out there, and Angel lay down beside him, with her head against his chest so that she could hear the deep, soft thunder of his heart. When he spoke it caused a soft vibration against her ear.

'What happened today has happened before. I

see him all the time, in crowds, at the end of streets, going into shops, only he's never there when I follow him. Because he never is there, except in my mind. Sometimes I think I'll spend the rest of my life chasing down endless roads that lead to nothing, or round and round in a maze that has no centre, and no exit.

'But even if I did find him, what good would it do? The money's gone. I'll never get it back from him.'

'You could hand him over to the police,' she suggested.

'For what? He didn't commit a crime. He just arranged things so that the debts fell on me. It was legal. I've got no comeback.'

It was true. For the first time Angel understood the sheer blank nothingness that faced him.

She was all he had to defend himself from that nothingness. And suddenly she was afraid for him.

# CHAPTER TEN

IN THE MORNING Angel made Vittorio breakfast in his minute kitchen, and they sat drinking coffee like an old married couple. They had passed the night in each other's arms, not making love, but being comfortable.

'Oh, by the way, we forgot these,' she said, rummaging in her purse and producing the lottery tickets. 'I'm not sure which one is yours any more.'

'It doesn't matter.' He took one without looking. 'When will we know if we're millionaires?'

'Tonight, I think.'

'What do you want to do today?'

'I don't mind, as long as it isn't energetic,' she said, smiling. 'And you're there.'

They spent the morning on the beach, doing nothing much except being sleepy and content. In the afternoon they bought rolls and wine and took them back to his shabby home, where they spent the afternoon in sleepy contentment.

'I could stay here for ever,' she murmured.

'So could I. But I suppose we have to go.'

'Back to the world,' she sighed. 'I hate the world.'

He kissed her forehead. 'Come on, let's go.'

They arrived at the villa to find Sam in good spirits and Berta about to serve the evening meal. Watching Vittorio across the table, Angel was happy to see that he seemed relaxed, as though their peaceful time together had wiped out the despair of the day before.

'Sam seems to have enjoyed his weekend,' she observed quietly to Roy. 'You were right about him needing his television.'

'He's got all tonight's programmes marked out.'

'Well, I want to watch the lottery programme.'

'Have you had a flutter?'

'You bet. I'm probably a millionaire by now.'

'Let me get you another coffee,' Roy said with comic deference.

'Maybe a multi-millionaire,' she teased.

'In that case, two coffees and some cake.'

'Vittorio's got a ticket too,' she said, laughing. 'It would be a shame for you to waste your energies buttering me up if he's going to be the millionaire.'

Frank's eyes gleamed. 'Vittorio, old friend,' he declared, 'why have I been neglecting you?'

Vittorio grinned, enjoying the joke, and everyone laughed. Sam declared that they would all watch the programme together, and at nine o'clock they gathered in front of the television. Even Berta and the maids crept in, refusing to miss the excitement.

'What numbers are we looking for?' Sam demanded.

They obediently read out from their tickets, and the opening credits of the show came up.

'Quiet everyone!' Sam insisted.

Almost at once it was clear that Vittorio had no hope, but Angel grew tense. The first number was hers, then the second, and the third, the fourth...

'What do you need?' Sam demanded in a stage whisper.

'Fifty-four and eighty-seven,' she said, hardly able to speak.

'*Fifty-four!*' came booming from the set, and everyone held their breath.

And the last one...

'*And finally, the number you've all been waiting for...*'

'Get on with it,' Sam begged in agony.

'*Eighty*—' There was a collective intake of breath from everyone in the room.

'Eighty-*nine*!'

The intake turned into a groan of disappointment.

'So near and yet so far,' Frank mourned.

Berta was the first to recover. 'But signora, you will still be a winner—not millions, but you have five numbers. The last man who had five received twenty-thousand euros.'

'In that case,' Sam yelled, 'let's have some champagne.'

'Twenty thousand,' Angel murmured.

The next moment she grabbed Vittorio's hand and dragged him out into the garden.

'Twenty thousand,' she said ecstatically. 'You can get out of that dump where you live.'

'But this money is yours.'

'No, it's ours. We bought the tickets together.'

'You bought them.'

'But you paid for your ticket,' she argued.

'It was your ticket that won.'

'Who's to say? I don't even remember which numbers I picked for yours or mine, and then the tickets got dropped in the carriage, and there's no way of knowing which one belongs to who. You're probably the real winner.'

The look he gave her was as gentle as it was implacable, and she knew that she'd done this all wrong.

'We divided the tickets and the winning numbers are yours,' he said quietly.

'But I want you to have this money. You need it.'

His voice was suddenly iron-hard. 'Understand me once and for all, I will not take your charity.'

'It isn't charity. I told you.'

'Yes, you were very clever in finding excuses to make me a gift of money, and if I had no pride I would let you.'

'Look,' Angel said, beginning to be desperate, for she could see she was against a brick wall. 'I do understand about your pride—'

'No, my dearest, you don't understand at all. You think you do, but there's no way you can even begin to understand.'

'But this is me,' she pleaded.

'And you think I have no pride with you? You think I'd find it easier to take money from you than from anyone else?'

'No, I suppose you'd find it harder,' she said wretchedly.

'Thank God you at least understand something. My pride seems a contemptible little thing to you, but it's all I have. Let me at least keep that.'

'After I took everything else from you. That's what you mean, isn't it?'

'It wasn't you who robbed me, I know. But now my pride is in your safekeeping and you must protect it for me. Only you can do so, and, if you don't, then you will truly have destroyed me.'

She made a last effort.

'All right. Half each. That's fair.'

For a moment she thought she'd persuaded him, but then an iron curtain seemed to come down over his face and she knew how far apart they really were.

'Please, Vittorio…'

He shook his head, gentle but unyielding.

'Oh, damn you!' she said, in tears.

He managed a smile then.

'Yes, damn me,' he said, touching her face. 'I can't say or do any of the things you want. I'm like a man with a leg missing. You'd gladly offer me a crutch but I can't learn how to use it. You should forget me and find a nice, sweet-tempered man who can say everything you want to hear.'

'I don't want a nice, sweet-tempered man,' she said, exasperated. 'I want you.'

Vittorio even managed to laugh at that, but he was very pale, as though something was gnawing at him painfully inside.

'You'd better get back,' he said. 'You can't miss the celebrations.'

'Come with me.'

'No, I'd rather go home.' He touched her face. 'I'm sorry. I can only be the way I am.'

If he had shouted and cursed, Angel could have born it better than this sad resignation. It showed her something she had tried not to see. He had nothing, and she had everything that should be his, and perhaps the greatest love in the world would be too little to survive that.

He walked away around the curve of the house, without looking back. A moment later she heard his car starting up, then fading into the distance.

The next time she saw Vittorio he smiled and spoke to her pleasantly, but he wouldn't let her refer to the subject again. When she tried he remembered something he had to do and vanished to a far point of the estate. To the casual eye all was well between them, but she knew that an abyss had opened up. Or perhaps it had always been there, and she had refused to see it.

He still came to the house to play chess with Sam, but she felt that he avoided being alone with her.

One evening, as they were just getting ready for supper and laughing over one of Sam's more outrageous stories, Berta came into the room, looking concerned.

'*Signora*, there is a man to see you. I asked his

name, but he just says he knows you will be glad to see him.'

'And that's right, isn't it, doll?' said a voice from the doorway. 'I haven't forgotten you, and I just know you haven't forgotten me.'

Everyone turned to see the swaggering creature standing there as though he owned the world, but only Vittorio spoke.

*'Mio Dio!'* he said. '"Ghastly Gavin."'

A loud snort of laughter from Sam greeted this, while Roy and Frank smothered grins. Gavin wisely pretended not to notice. It gave Angel a moment to get over her first surprise and study him.

She'd thought she knew how he looked, but the magazine pictures had only partly prepared her. He was heavier, flabbier, with an unhealthy, pasty face that spoke of self-indulgence. At nineteen she had thought him fantastically gorgeous. Now there was just enough of that Adonis left amid the ruin to make her sad.

'Hello Gavin,' she said.

'Angel!' He approached her with his arms outstretched, voice throaty with emotion. 'It's been so long.'

'Yes, hasn't it?' she said with faint amusement, before being swallowed up in an embrace that was so heavy with the cheapest brand of male cologne, nearly making her choke.

'Sam!' Gavin turned on him with even more fulsomeness, ready to embrace him too, but Sam was ready for him.

'Get off!' he spluttered. 'Who are you? I don't know you.'

'Of course you know me. We used to be the best of friends.'

'No, we didn't. I don't know you. And I don't like you.'

'Sure you do.'

'Don't you tell me what I like, young man. Keep away from me. You smell like a brothel.'

Gavin's smile became a little frayed and Angel, deciding it was time she remembered her duty as hostess, hastily introduced Roy, Frank and Vittorio as 'family friends'.

'It's lovely to see you again, Gavin,' she lied. 'But how do you come to be here?'

'I was just passing and I knew my old friend Angel lived nearby, so I thought I'd drop in.'

It was so absurd that Angel almost laughed out loud, but instead contented herself with saying, 'When you knew me I was Angela. I was never Angel to you.'

'But I always thought you were an angel,' he riposted quickly. 'Do you think you and I could talk—privately?'

He invested the last word with a throaty

emotion that was almost too much for her self-control.

'I'm afraid not,' she said firmly. 'We're about to have something to eat, but you're welcome to join us.'

'He damned well isn't,' Sam growled.

'Come on, Sam,' she coaxed. 'He's our guest.'

'He's no guest of mine. I don't want him in the house.'

'But it's Angel's house,' Gavin said, smiling ferociously.

'I wonder how you knew that,' Vittorio mused aloud to no one in particular. 'You must have been reading glossy magazines.'

'Throw him out,' Sam yelled.

'I can't send a guest on his way without something to eat,' Angel protested.

'All right, give him something to eat. Then throw him out.'

From the hall there came a cry and the sound of crockery hitting the floor. Angel turned to leave the room, but she was met at the door by Berta, who was flustered and annoyed.

'*Scusi, signora.* Ella has had an accident in the hall and broken some plates, but it was not her fault as she fell over two suitcases that she didn't know were there.'

'No, of course it wasn't her fault. Give Ella a

glass of wine and tell her to sit down for a while.'

They had spoken Italian but when Angel turned back to face Gavin it was clear that he'd understood the gist.

'I brought a few things with me,' he said with a placating air. 'I thought you might ask me to stay.'

'*Two* suitcases?' she enquired sweetly.

'I'm a snappy dresser.'

'Throw him out,' Sam protested.

'Gavin, I'm sorry I can't invite you for a long visit, but you can stay tonight.'

'No, he can't.' Sam sulked.

'One night will be just fine,' Gavin said. 'It's enough for me just to see you again.'

'I'm going to be sick,' Sam announced loudly.

Vittorio met his eye and winked.

Dinner was a fraught business. Angel's attempts to persuade Sam that he would rather eat in his room had met with a blank refusal.

'Well, don't sit there being rude to him all evening,' she begged.

'Why not? I never liked him.'

'You said you didn't remember meeting him before.'

'I don't. Aha! But you say I did,' Sam replied.

'Oh, you're so sharp! Yes, you did. I was dating him before I met Joe.'

'Well, there you are, then. I told you I never liked him.'

She waylaid Vittorio to say, 'I hope you're planning to stay.'

'Are you joking? I wouldn't miss this for anything.'

'You realise you started the problem with that "Ghastly Gavin" crack.'

'It's no crime to tell the truth. And I'm fascinated to discover what your taste used to be.'

'I was very young then,' Angel said defensively. 'And he was a lot slimmer.'

Vittorio grinned.

'Just help keep Sam in order, please. There's no knowing what he'll say tonight.'

'Really? I'd have thought we could guess exactly what he'll say. And no power on earth will stop him.'

In the event the evening was so dire as to be almost entertaining. Sam expressed himself loudly and often, ignoring all attempts to shush him. Vittorio, Angel noted with exasperation, was actually encouraging him.

Only Gavin seemed oblivious to the darts headed his way. He had set himself to play the part of a much-loved old friend whose visit was a matter for rejoicing, and nothing was going to divert him. It didn't matter that the audience was unresponsive and the performance fell flat. It was the role he'd prepared, and he stuck with it.

But he wasn't the only one playing a part. As the meal ended Sam grinned at Vittorio and said knowingly, 'You're drinking well tonight, my boy. I've never seen you putting it away like that.'

Since Vittorio had been notably abstemious that evening, everyone stared at this, except Vittorio himself, who said, 'Sorry, Sam. Do you think I've had too much?'

'Too much to be driving home along a cliff road. You'd better stay here tonight. No problem about that, is there?' This was to Angel.

'No problem at all,' she said, appreciating these tactics, and thinking that Sam could sometimes be more shrewd than anyone guessed.

All Gavin's cleverness wasn't enough to have Angel to himself. After supper Vittorio pinned him down to talk about motor cars, which Angel interrupted just long enough to say goodnight, before vanishing.

Then Roy and Frank emerged from putting Sam to bed, and suggested a nightcap. One brandy became three, then four. Gavin was finally assisted to his room by Vittorio, who dumped him on the bed before retiring to spend the rest of the night on a window seat from which he could see Gavin's door.

Gavin finally secured a private moment with Angel after breakfast the next morning, but this was less because of his own efforts than because Angel, exasperated, had decided to get it over with so that she could be rid of him. So she led him out onto the terrace.

'I thought we'd never be alone,' he said, in what he fondly hoped was a winning voice.

'Well, we're all rather busy.'

'I can see that, but I don't have to go immediately. If we could only spend a few days getting to know each other again…'

'Sam would never agree to that.'

'Sam's very protective of you, and I don' blame him.'

'That's good of you,' Angel replied, suppressing a desire to laugh.

'He remembers how close we once were.'

She was about to remind him that Sam didn' remember him at all, but decided not to bother. There was no diverting him from his self-deception, and the sooner he got to the end of his prepared script the better.

'You know, Angel, you really hurt me with those things you said in the magazine.'

'I hurt *you*? What about all that stuff you spouted about me dumping you for Joe? You know we'd finished before then.'

'Had we? That's not how I remember it. We were in love.'

'I thought we were. Then you wanted me to abandon Sam in a home, and that was that. I dumped you instead.'

'*Scusi, signora.* I have come for the coffee cups.'

With an oath, Gavin turned to see Vittorio standing just behind them.

'There are no coffee cups,' Angel said.

'Are you sure? Berta said—'

'There are no coffee cups!' Gavin bawled. 'Clear off.'

'*Scusi, scusi.*' Vittorio withdrew, apparently despondent.

Gavin took a deep breath and did his best to get back on track.

'I think you do me an injustice,' he said.

'Well, you got your revenge in that "heartbroken Gavin" piece. I hope they paid you well for it.'

'Probably less than they paid you to disparage me in *GlamChick*.'

'I didn't exactly disparage you. I just said your conversation was limited.'

'That's not all you said was limited,' he said, aggrieved.

'They made most of it up. Look, Gavin, the past is the past.'

'Sure it is. What matters is the future. When I saw those pics of you, looking so beautiful, I realised that I'd never stopped caring about you. You and I were good together—'

'And this is a lovely house.'

'What?'

'You saw the pictures of this house and thought you'd move in on me.'

'You do me an injustice.'

'You said that before. Well, I did say your conversation was limited.'

'Look, I understand you're playing hard to get. We've been a long time apart, but now we've found each other again—'

'Gavin, listen, we haven't found each other. It was over long ago, and it's still over—'

'You don't mean that—'

'*Scusi, signora*—Berta says—'

'Will you get out of here?' Gavin roared, confronting Vittorio, who had appeared like a genie from a trapdoor. 'Clear off! Do you hear me? Clear off, clear off.'

'*Scusi?* Me no spikka da English.'

Angel hastily placed a hand over her quivering mouth.

'What are you talking about?' Gavin raged. 'Last night you—why am I arguing with you? Buzz off!'

'*Scusi?* Buzz…?'

'Clear out! Buzz off! Get lost!'

'Happy to,' Vittorio said affably. 'But you're coming with me.'

Before Gavin could retreat, Vittorio reached up and took his ear between finger and thumb.

'*Leggo of me! Whaddaya think you're doing?*'

'Helping you on your way,' Vittorio said with deadly affability as he moved to the door, forcing the wriggling Gavin to follow.

'*Get off me!*'

'Our friend has decided to leave us,' Vittorio said, as if he hadn't spoken. 'Could somebody bring his luggage down?'

It was only then that Angel realised there was an interested audience that consisted of just about everyone in the household, led by Sam, who was acting as though Christmas had come. His eyes were bright with pleasure, and as he followed Vittorio and his squirming captive outside he was actually applauding.

'Vittorio, what are you going to do?' Angel said, half laughing, half anxious.

'Nothing sinister. Like a good taxi driver I'll take him into town and drop him at the bus station.'

Gavin opened his mouth to protest but a look from his captor silenced him. Vittorio's mouth might be smiling but his eyes were not.

'You can drop him at the station but you can't make him get on a bus,' she pointed out.

'Don't worry about him coming back. Along the way I'm going to explain to him how unwise that would be.'

'Then take someone else in case he puts up a fight.'

'Please, *signora*, do you really think I need help against this creature? Don't insult me.'

'That's right, don't insult him,' Sam echoed.

Having reached the car, Vittorio opened the back door, propelled Gavin inside and locked him in. Angel watched, appalled and fascinated, as Gavin hammered fruitlessly on the windows and shouted abuse that nobody could hear.

'Like a spider trapped in a bottle,' Vittorio observed dispassionately. 'And he isn't unlike a fat, bloated spider.'

Frank and Roy had hastened upstairs to Gavin's room and now emerged with his luggage, which they put in the trunk. As the car vanished they all waved at Gavin staring out of the rear window, still evidently wondering what was happening to him.

'What did he think he was doing?' Roy demanded.

'He thought it would be nice to come here and take over,' Angel said. 'And he thought I'd be stupid enough to fall for his line. That's the bit I can't forgive.'

'Well, Vittorio took care of him,' Sam rejoiced. 'I knew we could rely on him.' He was almost dancing with joy.

When Vittorio returned several hours later, Sam was the first to greet him.

'He won't come back, will he?' he asked anxiously.

Grinning, Vittorio tapped the side of his nose, but did not speak.

'That's right,' Sam agreed, nodding wisely. 'Don't tell us where you buried him.'

'Actually I just put him on a bus to Naples,' Vittorio said. 'Sorry to disappoint you.'

'I suppose it'll do for now.'

'Will you two listen to yourselves?' Angel demanded. 'Actually, I could have coped with him.'

Vittorio and Sam looked at her, then at each other. They shook their heads.

After that Sam was quiet for a few days. Sometimes he seemed to be sunk so deep in thought that Angel had to speak to him several times before he knew she was there, but this was different from his usual vagueness. Now she had a feeling that there was a purpose to his reveries, but when she tried to get him to open up he smiled brightly and told her not to worry her head about a thing, just as though she was a child again.

One morning he gave everyone the slip and went for a solitary walk in the garden. For a while he strolled apparently aimlessly, but when he saw Vittorio hard at work, pruning an apple tree, a sense of purpose seemed to envelope him, and he stepped out smartly, waving his stick and calling out.

Vittorio greeted him with a cheerful grin. 'You managed to escape, then?'

'Of course I did. That granddaughter of mine is a wonderful girl, but she does fuss so.'

'That's women for you,' Vittorio agreed wisely.

'The thing is that you have to let them think they're running the show,' Sam confided. 'Never let them suspect that you're really pulling the strings.'

'What strings have you been pulling now?'

'I've been thinking about that Gavin creature.'

'A nasty, slimy piece of work,' Vittorio agreed.

'But you knew how to deal with him. You're a man who can be relied on, and I've been thinking…' His voice trailed off and his eyes suddenly became unfocussed.

'Sam!' Vittorio said urgently.

'Ah, yes, where was I?'

'Thinking.'

'Ah, yes. I do a lot of that. People think I can't think, but I can. I've been writing my will. It's quite a document.'

'I'll bet it is.'

Sam fumbled in his pocket and brought out a sealed envelope, which he held out.

'Is this it?' Vittorio asked, taking the envelope. 'You want me to look after it for you?'

'That's right. Because you're my heir.'

'Oh, no—' Vittorio tried to hand it back but Sam became agitated.

'You must keep it because—because I've left you my most precious possession.'

'But surely that should go to Angel? She's the person you love.'

'You don't understand—my most precious possession—you must—' Sam sat down suddenly, gasping.

'Don't get yourself upset,' Vittorio said worriedly.

'You must take it—otherwise I can't feel safe—'

'All right.' He shoved the letter into his back pocket and looked anxiously into the old man's face. 'Are you feeling bad?'

'Just a bit—short of breath,' Sam gasped. 'I'll be all right in a minute.'

'I don't think so,' Vittorio said anxiously. 'Let's get home quickly.'

He pulled Sam's arm about his neck and raised him off the ground as easily as though he weighed nothing. Carrying him thus, he hurried to the house, calling Angel's name.

# CHAPTER ELEVEN

IT WAS QUIET in the hospital corridor. Vittorio pushed the door open slowly and looked into the room where Sam lay connected to machines. Beside him sat Angel, her whole attention fixed on the old man, so that she wasn't aware of Vittorio until his hand dropped lightly on her shoulder.

'Any change?' he asked.

'No,' she said in a despairing voice. 'He just lies there without moving. If only he could open his eyes and see me.'

'He had a massive heart attack,' Vittorio reminded her. 'He nearly died there and then, but he's still alive, and that's a good sign.'

It was thirty-six hours since Sam had been rushed into the hospital after his collapse. At first it had seemed as though nothing could save him, but the doctors and nurses had fought hard, and had finally made his condition stable. For the moment that was as much as could be hoped.

Since then Angel had stayed there, refusing to leave Sam's side, except when asked to move so that he could receive attention. Then she would flatten herself against the wall, almost invisible but never taking her eyes off him, until she could move back.

'Have you had any sleep?' Vittorio asked now.

'How can I sleep? I daren't. That might be the moment when…' She shuddered. 'When he opens his eyes,' she finished firmly.

'What about Roy and Frank? Can't they relieve you?'

'I've sent them away. They've hardly had any time off since they arrived, and Sam won't need them while he's here. So I said they should take a few days' holiday.'

Vittorio sat down on the other side of the bed from where he could partly see Angel's face. In such a brief time she had become thinner, and drawn. If she'd looked at him he would have reached out and taken her hand, but she seemed barely aware of him, and he wondered if he himself was to blame. If there was a distance between them now, who but himself had set it there?

'Berta packed a bag of overnight things for you,' he said. 'I left it there by your foot.'

She gave him a brief smile. 'Thank you.'

Night was falling. A nurse entered, checked the machines, spoke a quiet word to Angel, and departed. They sat in silence for some time until something about the angle of her head made him lean closer, and discover that she was asleep.

He immediately fixed his attention on Sam, silently taking over her vigil, not moving until two hours had passed and Angel suddenly jerked awake.

'*Sam!*'

'He's all right,' Vittorio said. 'I've been watching him. I'd have awoken you if there'd been any change.'

'Thank you.' Seeing him rise to his feet, she added, 'Yes, you go home now and get some sleep.'

'I'm just going to get you a coffee,' he said.

He returned with refreshments for two, and she devoured hers, famished.

'Can you remember when you last ate?' he asked tenderly.

She shook her head, before draining her coffee.

He immediately went to the machine to replace it, returning also with a bottle of mineral water and some fruit, which he set beside her.

'For later.'

'Even Berta doesn't look after me as well as this,' she said gratefully. 'But you must be tired. You don't have to stay.'

'No, I don't have to,' he said quietly, and sat down.

She smiled. 'Thank you.'

After a while she said, 'I didn't get the chance to ask you what happened when he collapsed. How did you come to be alone with him in the garden?'

'He came out to see me.'

'Without Frank or Roy?'

'I think he enjoyed giving them the slip. He was like a kid let out of school.'

'Yes, he's sweet when he's in that mood. I remember playing truant once, and he caught me, and instead of being angry he was full of plans about running away and never having to go to school again. Then, of course, I began to see how impractical it was, and decided to go back.'

'Which was what he'd meant all the time?'

'Of course. He's always so clever about things like that. Go on telling me what happened.'

'We had a chat, then he started gasping, so I brought him in.'

'What were you talking about?'

'Oh, this and that, silly things, nothing much.'

Inwardly Vittorio cursed himself for his own clumsiness. He could hardly tell her that Sam had been planning to make him his heir, even though it had been no more than a fantasy. Yet when he tried to think of something else his mind seized up, no ideas would come, and he was reduced to 'this and that'.

But, to his relief, Angel didn't seem to notice anything unsatisfactory about his answer, and soon she nodded off again.

She'd moved her chair further up the bed, so that she could rest her head against a chest of drawers, giving him a better look at her face. Angel had largely disappeared, leaving behind a woman who was a stranger to glamour. Her figure slumped inelegantly, her face was exhausted and ravaged by fear and grief. She was closer to plain than he had ever seen before, and his heart was wrung for her. He had to fight an impulse to take her into his arms, and draw her head onto his shoulder so that she might find rest with him.

He didn't yield, but he couldn't resist the temptation to kiss her, doing it so gently that her sleep was not disturbed.

They lived like that for two days. For all that time he acted as her servant, fetching and carrying for her, returning to the villa and bringing her back meals from Berta. Because Vittorio stood watch she was able to snatch precious hours of sleep.

As the time passed without Sam regaining consciousness Vittorio could see in Angel's face that she knew what was to happen.

'It's been so long,' she said sadly. 'I think I

could just about bear losing him if only he would wake and speak to me, just once.'

'Will that really make so much difference?' he asked, for he was afraid for her. 'He knew how much you loved him. Isn't that what really matters?'

'I know that's the sensible way to see it, but I long so much for a few more minutes, just to look into his eyes and know it's really him.'

'Have you tried talking to him?'

'I did at first, but what's the use? He can't hear me.'

'How do you know? They say hearing is the last sensation to go. He might be able to hear everything. Talk about your childhood, remind him of that time you played truant. Say anything, so that he can hear your voice.'

For hour after hour Angel leaned close, calling back moments from her childhood that she hadn't remembered for years. As she did so it seemed to her that the whole of their time together was being relived there in that quiet room.

Sometimes Vittorio slipped away to give her privacy, but sometimes he stayed because he couldn't bear to leave. In those hours he felt he learned more of her than ever before, and gradually a picture built up in his mind of the lonely, hurt child she had once been, and the old man who had overturned his life to make her happy.

He began to see Sam as he had once been, a trickster, a wit, a loveable idiot, and the most generous, great-hearted man who had ever lived. He understood now why she had repaid the debt, overturning her own life to make his last years happy. And he knew that if Sam died without speaking to her, he would feel her pain as his own.

She was asleep when the moment came. It was Vittorio who, watching closely, saw the first flutter of Sam's eyelids and nudged her.

'Wake up,' he said urgently. 'Angel, *wake up*!'

'What—?'

'Look at his face,' he said, full of joy for her.

There was a long moment when the two of them held their breath, then Sam's eyes opened. He was looking straight at Angel.

'Sam,' she breathed. 'Darling Sam. Thank goodness you've woken up.'

Vittorio slipped out to call the doctor.

'Woken—up?' Sam murmured.

'You've been unconscious for days, I thought you'd never wake.'

'Where am I?'

'In the hospital, in Amalfi.'

A long silence. 'Where?'

'Amalfi—you know, where we live now.'

In the long silence she thought she understood

the worst. Even so she wasn't prepared for the blankness in his eyes as he said, 'What are you talking about? Who are you?'

'But you know me,' she said frantically. 'I'm Angela. Please, please say you know me.'

'But I don't know you. I've never seen you before. Who are you?'

Vittorio, returning with the doctor, heard her desperate cry of *'Sam!'* and came in to find her lying with her arms around him. But Sam didn't return her embrace. His eyes were closed again and his hands lay still on the bed.

Roy and Frank returned for the funeral of the old man for whom they'd had a genuine affection. Everyone in the house turned out to say goodbye. In the short time he'd been there, Sam had become a favourite.

Next day Angel drove the lads down into Amalfi and dropped them at the bus stop.

'I'm so grateful to both of you,' she said. 'I always knew he was safe in your hands, and that meant the world to me.'

She handed them each an envelope. 'A little bonus to show my appreciation.'

They exclaimed over the amount, but Frank said, 'Are you sure? It's a lot.'

'It's worth it to me. Goodbye both of you.'

Vittorio was waiting for her outside the villa.

'Are you all right?' he asked at once. 'You should have let me do it.'

'No, I owed them that.'

'Come inside,' he said, taking her hand.

She was glad. It meant she wasn't alone as she entered the house.

'Berta's prepared you a special meal,' he told her.

'Stay and eat it with me.'

She smiled over dinner and made cheerful conversation. Vittorio waited for her to talk about Sam, ready to do anything she wanted, but she seemed determined to avoid the subject.

She'd wept over Sam's death, but then dried her tears quickly, and had not cried again, even at the funeral. It struck Vittorio as unnatural. She'd loved Sam more than anyone, but now it was as though she'd made a decision to control her feelings.

At the funeral he'd thought how lovely she looked, being one of those women whose beauty was enhanced by black. But a shadow had settled over her face, and he guessed that it was there for ever now.

He took some plates out to Berta and when he returned Angel was no longer there. Instinct took him into Sam's room, and there he found her, in semi-darkness, looking around at the emptiness.

'I took such trouble to make everything perfect for him,' she said huskily. 'And he was here such a little time. I used to dream of our life, how I'd look after him, how close we'd be when I could really be with him instead of having to give Joe all my time.

'And then it was all over, and he died without knowing me. That's the bit I can't bear. I kept thinking we'd be close at the end, but he just asked who I was. Then he died, not knowing me.'

'He was a very sick man at the end—it doesn't mean he didn't really know you—'

'But it does,' she cried, her brave surface collapsing suddenly. 'He died a stranger, and I can't bear it.'

He pulled her into his arms, knowing that no words could help. It might be illogical that a few moments could count more with her than the happier times that had gone before, but he knew that logic had nothing to do with it.

He held her, stroking her hair and rocking slightly, until her sobs subsided. Then he said softly, 'Come to bed, and let's be together.'

Soon it would be the time for harvest. Every day they went along the tiers of lemons so that he could caress the fruit and sense through his skin when the right moment would be.

'Perhaps ten days,' Vittorio said once.

'It looks ripe to me.'

'But not to me. Trust me. Ten days. It'll be a fine harvest, and profitable.'

Angel longed for the harvest to be over. There were so many questions about the future, but they must wait until the work was done.

She knew what she wanted. Him. Always. It wasn't just the passion that made her body sing. That was wonderful, but she needed more. And he had given her more. Since Sam's collapse he had shown her all the tender consideration of a husband, always at her service, asking nothing for himself. Now she no longer doubted either her love or his.

It had to be marriage. To go on as they were, with him as her employee, was impossible. His pride would forbid it. But as her husband he would regain his rightful place as master of the estate. It was very simple, really. She had only to find the right time to ask him. For she guessed that the suggestion of marriage must come from her. That was another matter where his pride would prove awkward. But she no longer had any doubts that things would work out well for them. The way ahead was clear.

There was a brief interruption in the form of a phone call from a man called Gino Tradini, which she found almost completely incomprehensible.

'He seems to be a customer for our lemons, but he's decided not to buy any more,' Angel told Vittorio. 'At least, I think that's what he said.'

He grinned. 'Is he up to his tricks again? Don't let him worry you. It's nothing but a con trick to get the price down. He tries it on every year. Doubtless he thought he could fool you because you're new to the business.'

'Perhaps you should deal with him.'

'I will. But I'd better go and see him, and it'll mean being away for two days. He's some distance away.'

'Well, if it's the only way…'

'I'll go tomorrow.'

'Let's have an evening out first. There's a little fish restaurant in town that I've always wanted to go to.'

They dined on the waterfront, seated at the window where they could see the boats bobbing in the darkness.

'You look better tonight,' he said, smiling. 'More cheerful.'

'It's been so quiet and peaceful these last few days. You did that. You've left me nothing to worry about.'

'Good. That's how I want you to be. Don't fret about Tradini. I know how to handle his nonsense.'

'You told me once that I needed you on the estate, and I wouldn't listen. Now I know how true that was. What would I do if you went away?'

'That's not likely—unless you fire me?'

'No, I'm not going to do that. You might decide to leave.'

In silence Vittorio shook his head. He was looking at her with a smile of perfect understanding, and, with a surge of excitement, Angel knew that the moment had come.

'We could make it work, couldn't we?' she said, almost pleading. 'We've had so many difficulties in our way, but we've managed to put them aside. It's the future that matters.'

'Did you have any particular future in mind?' he asked carefully.

'Oh, yes, I have something very particular in mind.'

She looked at him with a question in her eyes, hoping that he would make it easy for her, but, still understanding her without words, he shook his head.

'You're not going to help me, are you?' she asked, almost laughing, so sure she was of her victory.

Again he shook his head, but now he too was on the verge of laughter.

'I can't,' he said. 'You might not be going to say what I hope you're going to say, and then think what a fool I'd look.'

'Couldn't you risk looking a fool, just for me?'

'Nope! *You* take the risk.'

It was no risk at all, and they both knew it. He was hers as completely as she could ever want.

'Do you want me to go down on one knee?' she teased.

Then he really did laugh, reaching forward and taking her hands to draw them to his lips.

'If you're sure,' he said. 'You were right about the problems, but—'

'We'll find the way around them.'

'Yes, we will. I know that now. If only—'

A crack of laughter interrupted him. Looking round, they saw a beefy young man standing there regarding them sardonically. Vittorio cursed under his breath, recognising Mario, the young lout who had taunted him in the shop the day he'd collected the magazine.

'Oh, it's you,' he said wearily. 'Go away!'

'Why should I go? The entertainment around here is great. I don't know when I've had such a laugh.'

'Do you know him?' Angel asked.

'I employed him once, and fired him for being useless,' Vittorio said.

'Just a little misunderstanding,' Mario said. 'I'm not clever, like you.' He regarded both of them, and his mouth twisted in a sneer. 'You managed it, then. That's really clever.'

'What are you talking about?' Angel asked.

'You don't know? *Signora*, this man is a clever operator. He knew what he had to do to get his property back, and he did it. Just how long did it take him to wheedle his way into your bed, and how long—?'

The last words were choked off by Vittorio's hands around his throat. It took three men to pull him off.

Mario got to his feet, gasping. 'You'll be sorry for that,' he choked.

'Get out,' somebody said. 'How long do you think we can hold him?'

Mario fled.

'All right, let me go,' Vittorio snapped.

Cautiously they released him. His face was deadly pale, but he was in command of himself now.

'Let's go,' he said. 'Where's the bill?'

'I paid it,' Angel said. She'd done that quietly, so that they could get out of there without delay.

A strange look crossed his face. 'Of course you did,' he said.

Once outside Vittorio crossed the road towards

the beach and began to walk along it. His shoulders were hunched and he looked a completely different person from the happy man of only a few minutes ago.

'You really scared me,' she said, tucking her hand into the crook of his elbow. 'I thought you were going to kill him.'

'I might have done,' he growled.

'Why?'

'*Why?*' He turned to face her so abruptly that her hand fell away. 'Why? Did you hear what he was saying?'

'Yes, but so what? He's a cheap lout. Who cares what he thinks?' Then enlightenment dawned, or so she thought. 'You're not seriously worried that *I* think that, are you? Because I don't.'

'What he thinks, others will think,' he growled. 'And they'll say I played a cynical game to win you over and recover what used to be mine.'

'But *I* don't think it. The others don't matter because they don't know what's between us. But we know.' For the first time something in his manner made her falter. 'Don't we?'

He stood before her, the moonlight on his face making it livid.

'Do you remember how you once taunted me?' he asked. 'You said that you could play any part and fool me. "*I could say anything if I wanted to*

*How would you know the difference?*" Those were your words. And they were true. You boasted of having a dozen techniques. "*There's a way to make a fool of almost any man. You just have to find what it is.*'"

'And you're throwing that up against me now?' she whispered, horrified.

'No, I'm not. I know you well enough not to believe those words. But how well do you know me? Don't you realise that I might have the same skills? *I could say anything if I wanted to. How would you know the difference?*'

'Because I trust you,' she cried.

'Why? Because I told you that you could? Are you so sure I was telling the truth?'

'Don't!' she screamed, turning away, her hands over her ears. 'Don't try to turn my trust against me. Don't use my love as a weapon.'

'I have to, because it's the only weapon that can make you see the danger. Perhaps I'm sharper than you allowed for. I did it well, didn't I? I made love to you so cleverly that I even got you to propose to me, and I did it without once telling you that I loved you.'

Angel was silent, stricken. It was true that he had never said it.

'Are you saying that you don't love me?' she asked.

'If I said that I did, would you know it was true?'

In the long silence that followed she felt the wind begin to whip around her, with a soft, moaning sound. How cold it was suddenly.

'I thought I would—once,' she said slowly.

He put his hands on her shoulders, drawing her close and speaking with his mouth almost against hers.

'Do you know now?' he murmured.

With her head swimming, Angel realised that she knew nothing. He could tell her any lie and convince her. But she had already accepted the risk, knowing in her heart that he was worth it. Why couldn't he believe that about himself?

Or was it her that he couldn't believe?

'Vittorio—why are you doing this?'

'Because I can see the future,' he said simply. 'When we have our first serious quarrel—and we'll have it—it'll be terrible because there's a cruel devil in me.'

'I know,' she said softly.

'And I'll read in your eyes that you're thinking the same as the rest of them, trying to guess how many lies I told you to serve my own ends, wondering if you were a fool to trust me. And then I'll go mad.'

She stepped back sharply.

'Oh, you coward,' she breathed. 'You talk about

me trusting you, but it's you who can't trust me. It's funny, isn't it? Earlier we were talking about risks, and you said I must take the risk. Because you can't take one.'

'That's not what I—'

'No, it's not what you meant, but it's what I can understand. You're not the only one who can see the future. You've just shown it to me. I'm not afraid to risk everything, but you are. I'd have taken any chance with you, and trusted you through thick and thin, but all you see is your neighbours sniggering. Well, I tell you this, if their opinion is so much more important to you than mine—then to hell with you!'

'Angel, listen—'

'I've listened enough and you have nothing to say that I care to hear.' She took a step back. 'You warned me once that you could only do things on your own terms. I should have listened.' She sighed distractedly and ran a hand through her hair. 'Let's not talk any more now.'

'I'll drive you home.'

'No, I'll get a taxi. You have to start your journey early tomorrow, and when you come back—when you come back…'

'Angel,' he said, almost pleading.

'I told you before, don't call me Angel. It's not who I am.'

'Who are you?' he said slowly.

'I don't know. I thought I did, but you've made me see so many new things—things I don't like. I can't talk now. Goodbye.'

Angel turned quickly and walked away across the sand. At this moment she wanted nothing so much as to get away from him. She had told him that she could see the future. She saw it now, and it broke her heart.

# CHAPTER TWELVE

IT TOOK Vittorio two days to sort out Gino Tradini and get him to double his order at an increased price. As he'd suspected, the man had thought he could cheat Angel because she was new to the business. Vittorio took a bitter satisfaction in making it plain to him just how wrong he was. Then he drove home slowly, trying to decide exactly what he was going to say to her.

He had two speeches alternating in his mind. In one he told her that he agreed with her that they had no chance together. In the other he begged her to forget everything that had gone before, and simply love him and stay with him. He only wished he knew which one he was going to deliver.

But then he realised that he would know the answer only when he saw her.

As he neared the house he found himself looking for her, for she would surely be watching for him, and run to greet him. But there was only Luca, whom he had left here, and Toni. Together they swarmed over him, and he raised his voice to chide them fondly, thinking the sound would bring her out.

But there was no sign of her.

He went straight into the kitchen where Berta was making coffee.

'I need to talk to the *padrona* at once. Where is she?'

She stared at him. 'But—I thought you'd know. She's gone.'

'Gone where?'

'I don't know. Just gone. She left yesterday.'

'But she must have told you something.'

'She just packed her things and left. Wait—'

But Vittorio had already run out, heading up the stairs to her room. There he threw open the wardrobes one by one, finding each one empty. The drawers were also empty. There was nothing to suggest that she had ever been here.

He had returned half prepared to set a distance between them, but now the distance was there and it hit him like a blow in the face.

Berta came in to find him staring around at the bare room, his face ashen.

'Did she leave me no message, Berta?'

'She wants you to see this man,' Berta said,

olding out a card bearing the name Emilio Varini, partner in a firm of lawyers in Amalfi.

'That's all?' he asked, aghast. 'She sends me to a lawyer?'

Berta nodded.

'I'll go now,' he said grimly.

Signor Varini's office was on the waterfront. He was a small man, precise in physique as well as in manner. Vittorio had met him before when arranging a sale to one of his clients.

'I've been expecting you, Signor Tazzini,' he said. 'I have something to give you.'

'Where is Signora Clannan?' Vittorio asked without preamble.

'She did not inform me of her destination. She only asked me to talk to you, and give you this.'

He handed over a large envelope full of papers, which Vittorio spread on the desk. But the words danced before him and at first he could make no sense of them. When they did begin to form a pattern they conveyed a message so monstrous that his mind refused to recognise it.

'What is this all about?' he demanded.

'I think the meaning is clear, *signore*. The Tazzini estate is yours again. The Signora Clannan has signed it over to you.'

'What do you mean, signed it over to me?'

'She has given it to you. The property is now entirely yours once more.'

Still his mind refused to function.

'But she can't just—how much does she want for it?'

'She wants nothing. If you examine the documents you'll see that you are now the legal owner of the estate.'

'And you just let her do it?' Vittorio demanded, outraged. 'You let her give away everything she had?'

'I naturally advised caution, but I couldn't change her mind, and the property was hers to dispose of as she pleased.'

'But didn't she explain why?'

'Yes, she said she didn't need it any more.'

Now that Sam was dead, he thought with sinking heart. Why hadn't he seen this coming?

'It was an emotional impulse,' Vittorio said. 'How can anyone do business that way? Of course I cannot accept. Please contact her at once and tell her that.'

'But I can't do that. I don't know where she is.'

'Call her mobile.'

'She has changed the number.'

'Then send her an e-mail.'

'She's changed her e-mail address. I have no way of contacting her at all.'

'But that's impossible. What happens if there's an emergency?'

'That's what I said to her. But she said that she was cutting all ties with this place, and then it would be as though she had never existed. And if she didn't exist, there could be no emergency.'

The phrase 'cutting all ties' caused a dreadful sinking in his stomach. To avoid it Vittorio grew angry.

'Varini, listen to me. I will not accept this, and you must tell her so. You *must*.'

'I have no way of doing so,' the lawyer said with slow deliberation.

'I don't believe you. I will not accept that. After today I won't return there again. Tell her that.'

'Signor Tazzini, let me make the matter plain to you. If you don't accept the estate, then it will go into limbo. If nobody owns it, nobody can care for it. Nobody can buy seed or fertiliser, nobody can plant, nobody can harvest. The place will go to rack and ruin.'

'Harvest,' he said slowly.

'It's about now, isn't it?'

'Yes, we should be starting soon.'

He thought of the orchard, heavy with ripe fruit, waiting for loving hands to pluck the lemons, waiting in vain, rotting, useless.

'I'll take it back,' he groaned, 'but only temporarily. Find a way to contact your client and tell her to get back here.'

'If you'll just sign these papers,' the lawyer said.

When the last signature had been completed and witnessed, Emilio Varini reached into his desk and produced another sealed envelope.

'This is also for you,' he said. 'Signora Clannan said it was to be given to you only when you had formally accepted the estate.'

'Thank you,' Vittorio said in a dead voice.

Mechanically he put the envelope in his pocket, took his copy of the papers and left the office. He drove home slowly, his mind refusing to accept what was happening. Not until he was in the house and safely alone did he pull out the envelope and sit staring at it.

For a while he did nothing else. As long as he didn't read the letter it wasn't true, and with all his soul he longed for it not to be true.

When he couldn't find an excuse to put it off any longer he opened the letter.

My darling,
By the time you read this the estate will be yours again, as really it always was.
I think we both knew how it was bound to

end. I love you, but I can't live on one side of an abyss with you on the other. Nor can I cross the abyss to find you, because you won't let me. I can't reach the enclosed place where you live, and I can't spend my life beating my head against the wall. I would only end in hating you, and I don't want to do that. What we had only lasted a short time, but it was the most beautiful thing that ever happened to me, or ever will, and it must not end in bitterness.

This way there doesn't have to be bitterness, only the recognition that we didn't really have a chance. That's true, isn't it? I owned something that was rightly yours, and we could never get past that. I'd gladly share with you, if only you'd let me. But you won't, so there's only this way left.

I've tried to make you understand that I trust you totally, but you'll never believe it, and that gives us no hope.

The past few years have left me not knowing who I am. Now I want to go back to the turning in the road, and find my true self again.

I've left Toni with you. I can't take him with me, and I know you'll love him and care for him.

He crumpled the letter in his hand, turning around sharply as though he could discover a way out. She was wrong, he thought passionately. He knew her true self. It was the loving, generous woman he'd found in his arms, and then been fool enough to throw away.

But, whatever she said, it wasn't too late for them. Somehow it would be possible to find her and make her see that they belonged together.

He spread out the letter again, smoothing the creases, and it was only then that he saw the last lines.

My darling, please don't try to find me. This is something I need to do. I shall love you always. Thank you for everything.

It was signed 'Angela'. Not 'Angel'.

As he read the last lines again and again Vittorio knew that he had no choice. He must give her the peace she asked for. It was the only thing left that he could do for her.

Hardly knowing what he did, he went out into the hall and began to wander through the house, trying not to hear the empty way it echoed around him. A thousand times he'd told himself that he would never rest while the usurper was there. Now she was gone, driven out by harsh words and ruthless pride, and the place was his again in a triumph so total that he could never have imagined it.

He shivered.

The Ristorante Michelangelo stood in a small side street in the northern part of Rome. It was always busy, for the food was plentiful and cheap, and the wine good. To students of the nearby university it was a place to congregate.

To some of them it was also a godsend, providing employment that helped to keep them financially above water, but only the poorest needed to take up the offer. One face had caused a good deal of comment, but to the cheeky lad who had said, 'Hey, aren't you Angel?' she had replied simply, 'No, I was once. Not any more.'

That had been eight months ago. Nobody asked now.

Tonight it was late, her feet were tired, and she was glad it would soon be time to close. Just one more customer.

'What can I get you, *signore*?' she asked, suppressing a yawn.

'I've found what I came for,' he said.

She looked up from her pad, and paled. 'How did you find me?'

'It took a while,' Vittorio said. 'I tried the

English universities first, but then I realised you'd still be in Italy. Eventually I found you here.'

Somebody called her. 'I have customers to see to,' she told him.

'I'll wait for you outside.'

That gave her time to take command of herself. She was furious with him for disturbing her hard-won peace, but she could cope. This was the life she'd chosen, and even found some happiness in it. Now she could demonstrate, to him and herself, how complete was that victory.

Even so, when the time came to leave, she slipped out the back.

'I thought so.' Vittorio sounded pleased with himself. 'It's exactly what I'd have done.'

He moved out from where he'd been waiting, leaning against the wall. The light from a wall lamp fell directly onto him, giving him an eerie look in the near darkness.

'You'd have looked silly if I'd gone out the front way,' Angel said, trying not to let her voice shake. Even with the first shock gone, his impact was stunning.

'No, I can see the front door from here. You were never going to escape me. You did so once. Not again.'

As if to prove him wrong, she walked ahead, forcing him to hurry to catch up with her.

'Don't go so fast. We have to talk.'

'Maybe it's better if we don't.'

'Angel, wait—'

But if anything she walked faster so he raised his voice and called, *'Angela!'*

That made her stop and turn to face him.

'What is there to talk about?'

'Aren't you curious about why I sought you out? I wasn't going to look for you at first, but then something happened—it'll take me a while to tell you about it.'

'All right, I'll take you home. Just for a while.'

Her home turned out to be a tiny apartment at the top of a three-storey building

'It's a bit untidy,' she said. 'That's my room-mates.'

'You share this little place?'

It was the best she could afford, he realised. He looked around, thinking of the villa she had left, the property that had been hers. And now this.

They looked at each other for a moment, reading the lonely months in each other's faces.

Just by being here he made it look different, she realised. She'd come to this down-at-heel place when the university had accepted her, determined to make her precious little store of money last.

Here she'd fought her lonely battle, jumping every time someone came to the door, half hoping, half fearful, never quite knowing which one she felt more.

There had been temptations, times when she'd wanted to give it all up, run back to him, and forget everything else as long as they could be together, with love. But she'd fought back, using a mind that had received too little exercise, forcing it to expand, bending and hammering it into shape until it became a formidable instrument, and from somewhere she'd rediscovered the joy of learning.

It had proved all she'd hoped. With pleasure she had discovered that what happened inside her head could fight back against the loneliness of her heart and the aching need of her body. Not always, and not with finality. But the weapon, once discovered, could be used many times. With that, she'd made the most important discovery in life. She could cope.

And then he had to return, here where she'd won her battle, dimming it slightly with reminders of things she couldn't afford to remember, because then the battle would have to be fought again.

As if he could read her thoughts, Vittorio said, 'You made it, then. University, history of art, the academic life. Everything you wanted. Are you happy?'

'Yes,' she said, adding after a moment, 'Sometimes.'

'Sometimes,' he echoed. 'Yes, I know about that. I'm happy sometimes. I was happy when the harvest came in, the best there's ever been, the richest, the ripest, the most beautiful. It was your harvest too. Why weren't you there?'

'You know why. It was never my harvest.'

'I stood and watched the trucks rolling away with our produce, that we'd schemed and planned for. But then I realised I was standing alone, and that was the end of happiness. Look.'

He handed her an envelope full of photographs. It was all there, just as he'd said, an abundance of ripeness, beauty and success. Everything they had wanted.

'I'm glad,' she said, coming to the last picture. 'Oh, this one…'

It showed Vittorio standing there with Luca and Toni.

'Toni misses you,' Vittorio said. 'He makes do with me, but he's still yours, and he knows it. He hates being in that house without you, almost as much as I do.'

'Please, don't—'

'Once that place belonged to me absolutely,' he

continued remorselessly. 'Now your ghost is there, in every shadow. I can't make her go away, perhaps because I don't really want to.'

'Why are you doing this to me?' she asked helplessly. 'I was managing—'

'Yes, so was I. Managing. But it's not enough.'

'Why now, after all this time? Why come to find me now?'

'Because Sam told me to.'

'Vittorio, please, that isn't funny.'

'I'm deadly serious. You once asked me what Sam and I talked about just before he collapsed, and I told you it was about this and that. That was true, but there was more. He'd been writing his will and said he wanted to leave me his most precious possession. He gave me the will, I put it away and then forgot it when he got sick and died.'

'But Sam didn't own a thing. He had nothing to leave.'

'That's what I thought, but I was wrong. You asked to be left alone, and I was going to honour that—but recently, I was so unhappy without you that I—' he shrugged. 'I gave in. I decided to put my own need of you before your wishes. Reprehensible, but it's what people do when they love someone more than they can cope with. The way I love you.

'Even then I still wasn't sure. In some ways I'm a superstitious man, and I kept hoping for a sign to tell me what to do. You can laugh if you want to.'

'I'm not laughing. Sam was a great believer in signs. He said, if you knew how to look, something would always happen to show you the way.'

'He was right. I remembered his will. I'd put it away hastily and never thought of it again. I had to hunt a long time, but in the end I found it.'

He took out the paper and handed it to her. 'Read it.'

She took the paper in unsteady hands and read,

*Vittorio, I leave you my most precious possession—my darling Angela. You'll know how to take care of her as she needs. Sam.*

'Oh, Sam,' she wept. 'Sam!'

'You see,' Vittorio said. 'His last coherent thoughts were about you. He didn't die a stranger after all.'

'No,' she choked. 'He didn't die a stranger.'

He turned her face up to him. 'Why are you crying?'

'Because you've given him back to me. Oh, my love —'

Then she did throw her arms about him in the way he'd dreamed of on his journey here. He clasped her tightly, like a man holding on to recovered treasure.

'I've come to take you home,' he said. 'Our home. Yours and mine together. Without you it isn't a home at all.'

'Don't,' she whispered longingly. 'Part of me wants to with all my heart, but—my love, I've missed you so much, but at the same time I've discovered something that I've always wanted. I'm not sure I can give it up now.'

'Why should you have to give it up? There are other universities. We'll find one closer to home and you can continue your studies there. I don't want to take that away from you. I don't want you to lose anything that makes you *you*. But I want you to be mine as well. Surely that can't be impossible? And it's what Sam wanted. Doesn't that count for something?'

But in the next moment he backtracked. 'No, forget I said that. You mustn't say yes just to please Sam. I don't want you on those terms. If you'd rather stay here I'll give you some money to help you complete your education, and then I'll go away and not bother you again. I can always hope that you'll come to me one day, but it has to be on your terms.'

'There's no need for money,' Angel said shakily.

'No need? When you're working in that place for peanuts?'

'I don't have to stay there. I had a call from a magazine—'

'No,' he said fiercely. 'You mustn't take even one step back to that life. If you've really found your path you've got to stick to it, no matter what. Even if—even if there's no place for me.'

'Don't,' she said frantically. 'I gave you up once, but I don't know if I'm strong enough to do it again.'

'I want you willingly, or not at all. So, perhaps I should do it for you.'

Pulling out his chequebook, he sat at the table and scribbled.

'Take it,' he said. 'Don't be too proud.' He gave a frayed smile. 'We both know how fatal pride can be, but you're wiser than me. Let there be an end to pride.'

She took the cheque between nerveless fingers, staring at the large amount.

'Your share of the harvest,' he said. 'I still want you to come back to me, but if not—goodbye, my darling.'

He kissed her cheek gently, the kiss of a friend, not a lover, yet no kiss he'd ever given her had been more full of love.

Then he walked out of the room.

She didn't move. She was still staring at the cheque, knowing suddenly that another fork in the road had appeared. And this time she *must* make the right decision. He had waited for a sign before coming to her, but where was the sign to help her?

His footsteps were on the stairs outside. It was the sound that had haunted her dreams so often, footsteps, fading, retreating out of her life for ever, leaving emptiness behind. She had heard those footsteps so many times, and never understood until now.

The road forked ahead of her, but the footsteps led only one way.

'Vittorio,' she cried, coming back to life. *'Vittorio, wait!'*

He had almost reached the street when he heard. He stopped, not sure whether the sound was real or part of his longing. But the next moment it came again, followed by a door being flung open, feet hurrying down to him.

'Vittorio! Wait for me, my love—my love!'

Only half believing what he heard, he began to retrace his steps. He was dreaming—as he'd dreamed of this so often before.

The next moment he saw her flying down the

stairs towards him, her shining eyes full of the answer he sought. He opened his arms wide to receive her, and she flung herself into them, for ever.

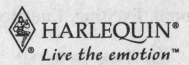

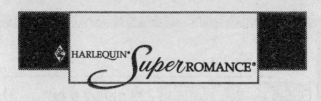
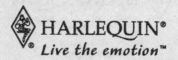

**Harlequin Historicals®**
Historical Romantic Adventure!

*From rugged lawmen and
valiant knights to defiant heiresses
and spirited frontierswomen,
Harlequin Historicals will
capture your imagination with
their dramatic scope, passion
and adventure.*

*Harlequin Historicals . . .
they're too good to miss!*

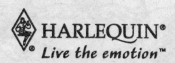

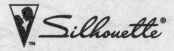